Final Bow

A Thriller

Book Ten in the Purple Frog Series

Harry F. Bunn

First published in 2023

All rights reserved. No part of this publication may be reproduced, stored in, or included in a retrievable system or transmitted in any form, or by any means, without the written permission of the author.

Copyright © 2023 by LifeMadeSimple, LLC

DISCLAIMER

Final Bow is a work of fiction. Although much of the backdrop and many of the locations are real, all of the characters are fictitious and purely conjured up by the mind of the author. In particular, the leaders of the United States, Russia, Iran, North Korea, and China are fictionalized characterizations and may not resemble the current leaders of those countries in any way.

Editing by J.H. Fleming
Formatting by Marissa Lete
Cover design by Daniel Eyenegho
ISBN 9798396143852

Dedication

Final Bow is the final book in the Purple Frog series, and over the past two-and-a-half years, I have written and published ten books in the series.

These have been my first at attempt writing fiction, and I want to thank all the readers who have embraced the stories and characters and provided valuable feedback.

On the journey, I have learned a lot about writing, much of it from interactions with other writers in the St. Croix Writers' Circle, and I dedicate this book to them. Thanks for your help, advice, critiques, and encouragement. Particular thanks go to Apple Gidley, who, until recently, led the group.

Over the past couple of years, I have met many people who feel they have a book lurking inside them. They have asked me what they should do about this urge, and my advice is just "write it." Find a style of writing you feel comfortable with and start writing. The journey starts with the first step.

A final dedication goes to my wife, Jackie. She does not normally enjoy thrillers, but has read the Purple Frog novels and says she loves them (and I believe her). Thanks for your love and support over the past forty years.

Harry F. Bunn,
St. Croix, USVI

The best government is a benevolent tyranny tempered by an occasional assassination.

Voltaire (1750)

Voltaire lived in France from 1694 to 1778.

He was a historian, a philosopher, and a versatile and prolific writer, producing works in almost every literary form, including plays, poems, novels, essays, histories, and scientific works.

He wrote more than 20,000 letters and 2,000 books and pamphlets.

Voltaire was one of the first authors to become renowned and commercially successful internationally. He was an outspoken advocate of civil liberties and was at constant risk from the strict censorship laws of the Catholic French monarchy.

Source: Wikipedia

Table of Contents

Prologue 1

Chapter One 3

Chapter Two 8

Chapter Three 18

Chapter Four 25

Chapter Five 38

Chapter Six 47

Chapter Seven 59

Chapter Eight 69

Chapter Nine 80

Chapter Ten 90

Chapter Eleven 101

Chapter Twelve 112

Chapter Thirteen 116

Chapter Fourteen 125

Chapter Fifteen 133

Chapter Sixteen 143

Chapter Seventeen 156

Chapter Eighteen 165

Chapter Nineteen 172

Chapter Twenty 181

Chapter Twenty-One	193
Chapter Twenty-Two	202
Chapter Twenty-Three	216
Chapter Twenty-Four	225
Chapter Twenty-Five	234
Chapter Twenty-Six	244
Chapter Twenty-Seven	254
Chapter Twenty-Eight	263
Chapter Twenty-Nine	272
Chapter Thirty	277
About the Author:	287

Prologue

The president's chief of staff beamed at the incumbent leader of the free world.

"Incredible news, Mr. President," he said. "Iran has agreed to stop their nuclear development and has requested international inspectors to verify their compliance."

The man continued as the president blinked in the early afternoon sun, which reflected off the snow on the lawn outside the Oval Office.

"There's more. North Korea has said they will do the same. That was without our solicitation."

The man was beside himself.

"And Russia, sir. Russia has communicated that they'll withdraw all their troops from Ukraine, including Crimea."

The man could not restrain himself from sharing the fourth piece of news with his boss.

"China has agreed that Taiwan should be reclassified as an independent country. They also said they will withdraw their troops in the South China Sea."

Bill Draper, president of the United States of America, settled down in his chair behind the Resolute Desk. The winter had been bleak, but today, the sun shone, and even through the bullet-proof glass in the windows, he thought he could feel the warmth. He was overcome with a feeling of well-being that he had never experienced before.

Then an irritating voice talked over his chief of staff. Draper attempted to understand where the voice was coming from and what it was saying. His mind became cloudy as he grappled with the new sound.

"Mr. President, it's 6:30 a.m. and you asked to be woken early today for your call with the Russian president."

He rolled over in his bed and rubbed his eyes. Sleet blew against his bedroom windows. *Damn!*

Chapter One

"You want us to do what?" Silvia shook her head. "Jason, are you out of your mind?"

Silvia Lewis looked around the office. It was modern with comfortable armchairs, a large desk, three computer screens, and two large screen monitors on the wall. It had no windows, and while large for a single incumbent, with three of them in the room, it seemed small. It could have been anywhere, but was located under Jason Overly's extensive house in St. Croix in the U.S. Virgin Islands.

The three occupants made up the senior management team at Purple Frog. Silvia was director of the clandestine spy organization, Alan Harlan was head of operations, and Silvia's boss, Jason Overly, was a retired technology billionaire who, twelve years before, had created the framework for their organization and funded its operation.

Jason looked at the other two and managed to retain a calm demeanor, resisting an urge to shout at them.

"I flew you and Alan down here," Jason said, "because what I have developed is something very special and very secret. I've spent a lot of time thinking about it."

Jason's housekeeper, Doris, had set up a drip coffee machine, which was half full of the dark brew. Silvia helped herself to a third cup.

Jason continued. "The Russians are fighting a stupid war, and sometimes losing a thousand troops in a day. Fewer Ukrainians are dying, but they're still losing hundreds. Both sides are in World War I trench warfare mode. One day, the Russians advance a hundred yards, leaving their dead all over the field, and the next day the Ukrainians win it back. More bodies."

He stood and started to pace.

"Since the beginning of Russia's 'special military operation,' nearly two hundred thousand on both sides have been injured or killed."

Silvia rolled her eyes. She knew all this.

Jason continued his rant. "In the meantime, the West has resisted sending the weapons that would allow a Ukrainian victory and Russia keeps threatening a nuclear response."

He stopped pacing and resumed his seat.

"The leaders in Washington and Moscow are playing it like a board game of Monopoly. But it's people's lives that are being squandered, not play money. Both sides have ruled out a negotiated settlement, so there'll probably be a continuation of the war for years, with humans paying the price. And beyond Ukraine, the world is suffering from the side effects."

He slammed his hand on the conference room table.

"My plan cuts through all that."

Silvia was still annoyed at what her boss was suggesting. "The U.S. and Europe are just attempting to keep the conflict contained."

He was incensed. "Really? Contained? Thousands are dying. I don't call that contained."

Alan had been quiet until now. "Your plan is certainly bold, Jason, but we've considered this approach before and always concluded that we might create a situation with an even worse outcome."

"We can't be sure of the end result," Silvia added, "and whereas our normal missions have clear objectives and are…" —she searched for the right word— "…contained, your plan interferes at a global scale. It would change the way the world operates. It may end up being better, but it might also be worse. The risk's too high. I can't support it."

Jason interjected, "Purple Frog has always had one goal and one goal alone: to foster world peace.

We've been successful doing that, but each of our operations has been tactical. We solve one issue and another rears its head. It's like whack-a-mole. My plan will consolidate all those missions and build something lasting."

Silvia shook her head and her boss, recognizing that his argument was failing, decided to change his approach.

"Let's get the Advisory Board's opinion."

"Jason, apart from you, there are only two people on the board. One is a judge and the other a retired think tank official. I'm not comfortable just relying on them for a decision of this magnitude."

"Then let's increase the size of the board. We'll recruit another four or five. Why not six?"

"Damn it. No. You want us to play God."

"We'll all share that role."

"I'm not buying it. If you keep pushing this, you'll have to find someone else to run it. I'm not doing it. I'll have to resign."

Jason Overly exploded. "Don't try that game with me, Silvia. Threatening to resign doesn't work. Over the years, others have tried to play that card and my response has always been to accept their resignation."

She shrugged. "Okay, I resign."

He threw up his hands. "Accepted." He turned to Alan. "You're promoted to director. Congratulations."

"Actually, I agree with Silvia."

"Then you had better resign as well."

"You're right. I quit."

Outside, the sun shone brightly, and the temperature had reached eighty-six degrees. Inside the office, it was chilly from the blasting air conditioning.

Jason pounded the table. "I'm surrounded by morons. This plan has the best chance of solving the most important of today's world problems: stopping the war in Ukraine. Not to mention the humanitarian and economic fringe benefits." He rose, calmed himself, and then quietly asked, "So, who is currently third in charge at Purple Frog?"

Chapter Two

It was early spring in the quiet Chinese city of Baotou, a conurbation north of Beijing and just three miles from the border with Mongolia. It was raining and gray, with a temperature just above freezing and gusting winds. Through the dark clouds, four large executive jets circled a military airport just west of the city, and in each, a head of state was accompanied by one or two bodyguards and one senior aide.

Dimitri Chekov, President of the Russian Federation, looked out of the small window at the desert, which stretched below for miles, linking with the Gobi in Mongolia. He shook his head. Yang, the Chinese president, had been insistent that he make the journey, with threats and offers of rewards. Yang wanted to meet secretly in this godforsaken place. Perhaps the Chinese planned to kill him, but the arrangements seemed too elaborate for that to be the case. If they wished him dead, Chinese fighters could have shot down his plane despite the two Russian MiG-35s which accompanied his jet.

He looked out again and observed, through the gloom, that there were three other executive jets circling the small runway, and above them, five or six fighter jets. He frowned. Yang had said there would be others at the meeting, but had not specified who. The fighters protecting these planes were too far away to see their markings, but Chekov guessed which countries they represented. If he was right, this was a historic meeting, and he now understood the rationale for the secrecy and the rule that only one aide was allowed to accompany him.

Although the aircraft came from diverse, far-flung locations, their pilots had been instructed to arrive overhead at the same time. The small control tower in the center of the landing strip communicated with each, coordinating the landing of the executive jets within a few minutes of each other.

Having touched down, the planes taxied to an area at the end of the runway, where seven armored Hongqi LS7 SUVs were parked, awaiting the group of world leaders. The fighters, which had escorted the aircraft, landed and started the job of refueling.

One hundred armed Chinese soldiers stood at attention, paying no heed to the heavy rain descending on them, and as the plane doors opened, they took up positions looking outwards, scanning the barren terrain for any possible threat. Bodyguards, also armed, descended from each aircraft and surveyed the setting before returning to the planes, soon emerging with large umbrellas, which they used to shield the leaders of Russia, Iran, North Korea, and China as they stepped down and approached one another. Each was accompanied by one aide, and the men regarded each other with suspicion, and in some cases, hostility.

"Truly a meeting of power." The North Korean leader looked at his fellows and gave them a watery smile.

A Chinese officer ran forward and beckoned for a half dozen Chinese aides, all holding large umbrellas, to advance on the visitors. The aides separated into three groups and bowed deeply to the visitors. The officer gestured to the Chinese leader, President Yang, who had arrived at the same time as the others.

Yang stood apart and had forsaken an umbrella. He wore a heavy overcoat and was drenched, but he stood erect. His position implied his seniority in the group, a stance that the visitors hated, but accepted.

The Chinese aides spoke to the visitors in their own languages. They wore headsets and welcomed the leaders on behalf of President Yang, speaking fluently and without marked accents. They explained that they were simultaneous translators and handed out wireless headsets through which the leaders would hear the translated words of the others.

Yang shouted out a few words which the interpreters translated. "It's wet out here. Please, enter the vehicles. We have one for each delegation and three additional for security. Our meeting building is close by. This is a historic moment. In the next five hours, we shall discuss a plan which will enable all of us to increase our global territories by perhaps half as much again."

The SUVs drove a mile to a compound circled by two sets of chain-linked fences and topped with razor wire. Tibetan mastiffs roamed in the gap between the fences, and the gate leading in and out of the facility was supplemented by ribbons of spikes on the roadway, which were rolled up to allow passage for the vehicles into the area. The occupants saw just one concrete building without windows in the compound, and it gave the appearance of being sunk into the ground of the Chinese countryside. Over one hundred armed soldiers held positions both inside and outside the site's perimeter.

The leaders alighted and were led to a door that opened as they approached.

"Looks like a bomb shelter," muttered Dimitri Chekov, the Russian president. The Russian was not in a pleasant mood, nor were any of the other visitors. Only Yang continued to smile and uttered encouraging platitudes.

The Chinese president led the way into the solitary building. There was no furniture and no partitioning. It was just one large room, but in the center was an elevator and entrances to steps leading downwards.

Yang had picked up on Chekov's comment and said loudly, "Yes, gentlemen. This is a bomb shelter, and we'll now take an elevator down to the most secure place on the planet so we can have our meeting in private." He laughed." Even if the Americans drop a nuclear warhead on us, we'll still be safe."

"I want one of these," Kim Ji-yoo of North Korea called out.

Yang entered the large elevator and beckoned for the other leaders to join hm. They did so and stood separate from one another, the elevator cage providing the space allowing them to do so. The door closed and they descended about two hundred feet. The door opened and they emerged into a well-lit and attractive area with expensive furniture and Chinese artwork.

A bevy of young women rushed forward with hot towels and offers of refreshment.

The elevator returned to the surface for the aides. The bodyguards were instructed to remain above ground, and although the visitors did not like this arrangement, they accepted it.

Yang took charge." We'll eat first and then start our business. You must be tired and hungry."

"I didn't come here for a Chinese takeout," the Iranian President stated flatly. "You're probably going to poison us." The Chinese aides translated his words into the various languages.

Hearing the Chinese interpretation of the Iranian's comment, the Chinese president accepted the rebuke, smiling." We have one of the best chefs from Beijing here today, and he is serving French cuisine with a slight Chinese twist. I'm told his food is excellent." He paused and then added, "If I wanted to kill you, my soldiers could have done that by now. Why would I resort to poison?"

They were escorted to a large round dining table as waiters emerged with drinks and the first course of their lunch.

Four courses were presented, and though it was excellent, as the president had suggested, there was little discussion as the atmosphere of mistrust and hostility continued among the world leaders.

Yang tried unsuccessfully to introduce a lighter atmosphere by offering small talk and avoiding any political or military topics.

"Did you enjoy traveling in private executive jets? Oh, you had your own fighter escort, but I wanted some animosity, and your normal presidential planes would have been too obvious."

"The jet you sent for me was too small. I am used to a much larger aircraft," Chekov said. He was still in a bad mood.

Yang scowled at the Russian, then turned to the others. "Fellow leaders, setting up this meeting was not easy. You each have a fundamental mistrust of each other, and I share that. Each of you has an ego the size of an elephant. But I managed to persuade you to come together and here we are."

Kim snarled. "I don't trust either of you." He gestured to the Russian and the Iranian. "But President Yang, you are my good friend."

The three continued to squabble, but finally, Yang had suffered enough and was annoyed that his attempt at an icebreaker had failed.

The meal had been served with traditional cutlery, not chopsticks, in an effort to make these powerful leaders more comfortable, and now Yang threw down his knife and fork onto the dining table.

"All right. End of hospitality. Let's go and get down to business."

The war room did not have a conference table. Instead, there were four large, comfortable couches arranged in a square to face inwards. Yang realized this would be a difficult meeting. However, he had a proposal to put to these men that he was certain they would embrace. Each leader, his aide, and an interpreter sat on one of the couches.

Yang remained seated but spoke forcefully. "Gentlemen, today we all have different agendas and different ambitions. But we have a common interest. We all regard the West as our enemy. Particularly America."

Chekov drummed his fingers on the edge of the couch. "Hopefully you have more substance than that. Flying here with all the secrecy and then being confronted with people I never thought would be in one room together is ridiculous."

The Iranian president, Farid Moradi, added, "I find it very unsettling to be in this group of leaders. None of you are Muslim, and I expect most of you don't even believe in God."

Kim laughed." And you do?"

"Yes. Allah is great."

"Enough," Yang said, temper flaring. "If all we do is squabble, this meeting will be a waste of time."

Chekov snarled. "Then tell us. Tell us what you have in mind."

The leaders settled down a little, but Yang was aware of the tension in the air.

He looked around and his eyes narrowed. He knew he was in charge, and the feeling pleased him.

"Fellow leaders, since before World War II, the United States has held a dominant place on the world stage. They have used their economic wealth to maintain that position and have forged alliances, many built on influence and aid payments, to create what we all call the West."

He saw they were paying attention.

"But the United States is a melting pot from the dregs of other societies. There are Germans, Poles, Arabs, Jews. A total mixture, while each of our countries has a purity of heritage going back millennia."

"We know all this, President Yang," Chekov said. "Get on with your pitch." He was clearly in a bad mood. The flight from Moscow had been arduous.

Yang picked up a remote device and triggered it. On huge screens around the room, the Chinese characters for the words quánqiú bàgōng were displayed, along with words in Farsi, Russian, and

Chosŏn'gŭl. Each leader read the words as Yang explained them. "Today, we are individual nations, but together, united, we shall be a Gang of Four. I'm going to tell you about an operation that I have called quánqiú bàgōng—Global Strike."

The chef and his staff served tea and Belgium chocolates.

Chapter Three

Yang rose and moved to the center of the couch arrangement. He turned and his eyes traveled around the room, fixing on each of his visitors in turn. "As I just said, we all have a common enemy: the West, but specifically the United States of America."

He looked around at the leaders and made a point of retaking his seat. He had their attention, and the interpreters paused, waiting for what he would say next.

"Each of you has a goal for what you, individually, want to achieve. Chekov, you want to occupy Ukraine and then Poland, and probably the Baltic states. You want to fracture NATO. You want to regain the power that the Soviet Union had in the seventies. You have chosen armed attack as your strategy. Invasion is your preferred instrument."

Chekov sneered. The summary had been accurate, but he resented being lectured on this by the Chinese president.

Yang turned to the dictator of the Hermit Kingdom. "Kim, you want to reunite all of Korea under Northern Korean control. Your strategy is to develop nuclear weaponry and a missile system that can deliver it. Your hope is that the South will capitulate, and your long-range nuclear missiles will intimidate the U.S. such that they choose not to help the South."

The interpreter was having some difficulty expressing Yang's message, but it was evident that Kim understood.

The Chinese president then addressed the president of Iran. "I understand why the Supreme Leader did not want to visit me here, but before we go further, I must be sure you have the authority to participate."

The Iranian answered, "Ayatollah Jannali has given me that authority."

As he spoke, four young women brought in more tea for each of the participants and refreshed the small cups on the tables next to each couch. The conversation did not pause as they did this.

Yang addressed the broader group and looked away from the Iranian. "Iran wants to follow a similar path to North Korea and use a nuclear threat to increase its position in the Middle East. Oh, and to destroy Israel."

The Russian president interrupted and spat out his words to the Iranian. "But, President Moradi, you are currently doing a deal with the Saudis. How does that play into your ambitions?"

Moradi half rose from his chair, obviously upset by Yang's statements and Chekov's question.

He turned to the Chinese president, ignoring the Russian." And what about China? What do you want?"

Yang tapped his fingers together. "I want territorial expansion, including but not limited to Taiwan. We in China are smarter than the rest of you. We have expansion strategies beyond military aggression. We shall attack our enemies with economic and cyber battles, not just military action."

As his words were translated, the leaders broke out into shouts, challenging Yang's statement about China's superiority.

The Chinese president continued. "But that doesn't matter. If any one of us challenges the West, they will fight back and cause huge economic turmoil and destruction. Russia has seen that in their stupid war in Ukraine. That war has been a disaster for Mother Russia."

Chekov sprang to his feet." I will not be spoken about like that."

Kim sprang to his feet as well, though it wasn't clear why he was doing it. Yang remained seated and laughed at the men in front of him.

The interpreters were in turmoil. They were trying to convey the tone as well as the words being uttered, but as they did so, the leaders shouted at them.

Yang continued his pitch. "So, fellow leaders, how successful have you been in your current strategies? Ukraine is a disaster. North Korea is spending a vast amount of money on nuclear weaponry, but the Americans are just sitting back and laughing. They could destroy your whole country within twenty-four hours if you launched an aggressive action against them. And Iran is in a similar situation, with sanctions destroying your economy and Israel thumbing its nose at you."

Yang waved his arms for the men to retake their seats and continued.

"In World War II, what did Hitler learn to his cost? That to fight a war on two fronts is a lethal error. Across the years, armies have been defeated when their attention is focused on more than a single battlefield."

He paused and sipped tea from his small cup.

"The U.S. and its voters are currently fully absorbed by the Ukrainian war. If you, Kim, started another battle on a second front, you might be successful. American resources would be stretched thin, and the American political parties would fight each other for the sake of scoring points."

Chekov glared at the Chinese president." So?"

Yang took another sip of his tea, increasing the tension and the curiosity of the other leaders. They waited to hear what he would say next. He spoke with confidence. "And now to Global Strike. What would happen if Russia made significant headway in Ukraine, North Korea launched an attack on Seoul, Iran bombed Tel Aviv, and we invaded Taiwan? At the same time. A gang of four against the West."

The others showed their astonishment at what Yang was suggesting, but he continued.

"If we launch our attacks at the same time, the West will need to face us in Eastern Europe, Taiwan, South Korea, and the Middle East simultaneously. They will be faced with fighting on four distinct fronts. It would be our Global Strike."

The room was quiet as each of the country leaders processed what Yang had just said.

Chekov broke the silence. "Are you saying you want us to all act together?"

The Chinese president nodded. "Yes. We will agree to a strategic alliance and each will launch significant simultaneous attacks on the West. Oh, the attacks might have a week or two between them, but the real value is that the Americans and their allies will be in turmoil as they decide how to allocate their military resources. Divided, they fall. We shall win and divide the world between us."

A hush fell over the room, and then a flurry of questions sprang up as the leaders expressed their views on Yang's plan. The discussion continued for another two hours as the various elements of the strategy were discussed and debated.

As the discussion died away, the North Korean summarized what they were all thinking. "This plan has merit, but it has enormous risk. We would be embarking on a path from which there is no return." He paused, then raised his head and looked about him. "But, acting alone will not accomplish our individual goals. I must think this through before agreeing to embark on this course." He did not add that adopting the plan required a level of trust between these men and that was far from present.

The others clearly felt the same way and Yang smiled. He had expected this. "Fellow leaders, I understand. But if you do not join our alliance, China will need to follow our ambitions separately and you will shift from being allies to, potentially, enemies. Do not make that error, my friends."

By the time his words had been translated and relayed to the leaders, Yang was ready to deliver his ultimatum.

"Take some time to think about this and make your decisions. But I want your answers within one week. Each of us has a lot to prepare before we launch our attack."

Chapter Four

On the other side of the world, in the office below his house—Sugar Ridge, in St. Croix—Jason glared at Silvia and Alan. He shook his head and threw up his hands in a gesture of surrender.

"Damn. I don't want your resignations. Let's work on this. The plan's simple. We'll assassinate Chekov and his top lieutenants and install someone who we, Purple Frog, control. We'll persuade the replacement to withdraw the Russian troops from Ukraine, and going forward, to concentrate his efforts on the internal Russian economy, not external aggression. He'll also commit to ceasing war efforts outside Russia's current boundaries."

Silvia shook her head. "So, Jason, you're saying we, in Purple Frog, should orchestrate a coup and then run Russia from our little headquarters in rural Virginia. Crazy. And very unethical."

Jason shrugged. "Why unethical? It's what Purple Frog's been doing for over ten years. You compromise someone in an enemy country and extort them to provide intel. In many cases, you have them take specific actions that we dictate. It's all within our quest for world peace.

"He continued. "What I'm proposing is just a step further. This time, we compromise a person who'll become Russia's president. In the past, we've tackled minor, tactical threats. This approach is strategic and will solve the bigger picture. I'm calling it Operation Switch."

Silvia was blunt. "You've lost it, Jason. Even if we agreed that this is a great idea and that it would solve the Ukrainian problem, implementing it would be impossible."

She sipped her coffee, then continued.

"President Chekov and his prime minister, Boda Morozov, are the most heavily-guarded men on the planet. Probably more so than the U.S. president. And even if we found a way to do it, whoever replaces them might be as bad or worse."

"Not if we decided who the replacement is, and we control him."

Silvia stood and walked over to the coffee machine. "Control him? How are we going to find someone who will accept what we are asking? How are we going to make him president? And if we could, he'll then have the power to do whatever he wants."

Alan decided to try another approach. "Do you have anyone in mind for the new president, Jason?"

Jason looked at him. "That'll require a lot of research and analysis, but one man who comes to mind is Boris Menklov."

Silvia let out a single laugh. "The oligarch?"

"That's him."

"Why him?"

"He has always been interested in the money, not the power. Chekov's war has already cost Russia hundreds of billions, and Menklov has personally lost several billion following the West's sanctions on him. He's even lost his prized yacht, which was impounded in Spain a few months ago."

Silvia refilled her cup. "There would be tremendous opposition from Chekov's allies. Russia is going to need a very strong leader to counter that."

"From what I know of Menklov, he'll get the rival factions in line, and quickly."

Alan chuckled. "He'll just kill them or imprison them."

Jason snorted. "Whatever."

Silvia sipped her coffee. "How would we control him?"

Alan stood and started to pace around the small office. "We already have certain leverage. Vivienne has a file on him. We were discussing him just a week ago. He still lives in Moscow, but he's old friends with Chekov."

Silvia put her coffee cup down. "Old friends? That doesn't bode well for him leading the coup."

Alan continued," They were in the old KGB together. They've fallen out over Ukraine, but still meet and discuss the old days. Falling out with Chekov usually means it's just a matter of time before the president's goons show him an open window in a high-rise, or he is jailed for corruption. He's smart, so he's still playing nice to Chekov, but my bet is that he's already planning an exit strategy."

Alan was starting to enjoy the discussion.

"He's a billionaire, but most of his wealth is in offshore accounts. Tyler and his money laundering people and Ching and his merry band of hackers could probably access those accounts."

Silvia was clearly still opposed to the idea. "But if he gets into power, won't he just tell us to get lost? He's not going to do everything we tell him to do."

Jason countered, "Our goal is, and has always been, to foster world peace. We won't try to interfere with Menklov's policies and actions within Russia, but we will insist that he stop external warfare. He'll need to pull Russian troops out of Ukraine and no longer threaten the West. The man's already given some vague hints that he would be in favor of terminating the war. His agenda is to save the Russian economy from its current death spiral."

Silvia shook her head. "His objectives might align with ours, but we'll need something more to persuade him to do what we want."

Alan looked up. "As I just said. We'll take over his bank accounts and we might be able to involve him in the assassination plot. If we have proof of that and we threaten his offshore accounts, he should find our deal attractive."

Jason assessed that Alan was coming around to his idea, but Silvia was still opposed. He continued, "It's unlikely to be a long-term solution, but we should be able to have him deescalate for four or five years. If so, we'll have made a major contribution. Over time, he'll have powerful people in Russia who'll demand external conquests, but he should be able to hold it together in the interim. The Ukraine war is incredibly unpopular in Russia. If Chekov's replacement pulls the troops out and negotiates for the sanctions to be lifted, he'll be well received."

Silvia said, "And what if he agrees to our requests and then changes his mind?"

Jason replied, "When I said Chekov would be removed, I was using a euphemism. We'll kill that son-of-a-bitch. Menklov will have the death of his predecessor uppermost in his mind, and we'll remind him of that."

Silvia seemed to decide it was time to make her position clear. "Jason, I'm opposed to this. Your arguments are interesting, and to some extent, persuasive, but I just can't go along with it." She turned to Alan. "Alan?"

He hesitated, then said, "I'm not sure on the ethics of the plan, but the practical aspects make it impossible. We haven't addressed how we'll remove Chekov and his deputy, nor how we'll put Menklov in power. And on that point, we need to research Menklov and other possibilities. He might not be the best choice."

Jason waved his hand in frustration. "Details, details, details."

The meeting was not progressing, so Jason decided to call a halt to it before it became too contentious.

"You'll want to think about this," he said. "Let's have lunch and then I'll have the jet take you back to Virginia."

The three emerged from the office that Jason called his bunker and blinked in the brilliant sunshine.

Doris, Jason's housekeeper and cook in St. Croix, excelled herself with a lunch of grilled local lobsters, and Jason unearthed a bottle of Sancerre that Alan declared was, "Outstanding."

Then Jason drove with them to the airport, and fifteen minutes later, they stood at the bottom of the steps leading to the aircraft. "No hard feelings?"

Silvia had calmed down." No, Jason. No hard feelings, but I still disagree with your plan."

"Noted. By the way, I had some drinks loaded for your return trip. A very nice Sauvignon Blanc for you, Silvia, and for Alan, a Talisker Storm." Storm was Alan's favorite single malt Scotch. Jason continued, "Actually, it's one I'd not heard of before. Talisker named this one Dark Storm. I'm told it's even better than Storm."

Alan laughed. "Thanks. It seems that Dark Storm might be a good name for what you are considering."

Ten minutes later, Jason watched as his personal jet lifted into the cloudless blue sky and turned to the northwest, taking Silvia and Alan back to Washington, D.C.

That night, Jason had a light evening meal and watched the news. The stories were like the ones the night before, and the night before that. The newscasters introduced new guests, who each had a slightly different twist to the story, but there was nothing new. He switched off the television and consulted his iPad, reading the vast array of news stories. He laughed as he read articles that described the public domain versions of some of the incidents or technologies that Purple Frog had been involved with. He read one about solid-state EV battery technology and Jason thought of November Swan. *I wonder where he is.*

It was a warm night, and he retired to bed at just after 10:00 P.M. and fell into a deep sleep.

Sometime after midnight, he experienced a dream, or rather a nightmare. It startled him, but he dozed back off again within a few minutes. He awoke fully at 2:00 A.M. and attempted to remember what he had experienced in the dream. The details were vague. He knew it foretold something bad, but he could not recall what that was. He remembered gushing blood, but whose blood, and what the flowing substance meant, he could not salvage from his memory.

Sweating, he rose, wrapped a bathrobe around him, and walked out onto the deck. The night was dark, and a sudden flash of lightning rippled through the sky. Rainfall was common in the islands, but it rarely lasted long. The showers were cherished by the residents, filling their cisterns and watering their vegetation. Lightning was rare, but tonight the sky was ablaze with it. Heavy rain descended on the house and Jason was caught in the downpour. The waning moon had set hours before, and the sky, usually full of stars, was hidden by dark clouds. A strong wind blew over the pool and up from the sea below.

He ignored his wet bathrobe and the rain and walked into the bar, where he poured himself a bourbon, adding a couple of ice cubes. The rain was easing, and a few minutes later it ceased. Turning on the pool light, Jason walked outside to a day bed, which was soaked, but he lay down anyway and looked up at the constellations, which were emerging as the clouds passed.

He thought of his dream and shook his head. *What did it mean?* He shrugged. *I'm being stupid. Everything is fine.* But the dream hovered in his mind. He drank down the fiery liquid and his mind shifted to his meeting with Silvia and Alan.

The retired technology billionaire trusted their judgment and took their concerns seriously. However, as CEO of Avanch, his technology company, he had decades of successful decision-making, and this provided him with confidence that Operation Switch was the right approach. The implementation would be difficult, but Purple Frog had faced challenges like this before and had always emerged victorious. Well, almost always.

He rose from the day bed, still soaked from the rain, and walked to the bar. He looked at the bourbon bottle and was about to reach for it, but stopped. *I don't need another*. His mind shifted to a dark area of his brain where there were doubts about the operation and a festering premonition of doom.

He needed some relief from his self-generated tension, and the next morning, as Doris was making his early espresso, he reached for his phone and made a call.

"Ben, old friend," he said when it was answered. "Care for lunch at the Yacht Club? My treat."

"Strewth, Jason, you must have some bloody great problem on your mind that you want to discuss. I don't think you've ever offered to buy me lunch before."

"That's bullshit." In fact, Jason had a reputation for being more than generous. "Today?"

"It works for me."

"One o'clock?"

"I'll be there. They have a new chef, and the dinner I had there last week was the bees 'knees."

Jason chuckled at his Australian friend's phraseology.

"Jason's buying. What's the most expensive drink you have?" Ben asked Stella, who was taking their beverage orders. He looked at Jason, then back at the waitress and laughed. "Never mind, love. I'll just have a Heineken."

Stella keyed in Ben's order and then took Jason's. She left them to prepare the beverages.

Jason felt a small wave of calm spreading over him.

"This club is so relaxing," he said.

Ben looked around. "Yeah. But don't you doze off, you old bugger."

After a quarter of an hour of small talk and a couple of drinks, they placed their lunch orders and Ben sat back, looking his friend up and down. "You're bloody stressed out, aren't you?"

Jason nodded. Ben knew him well. "I can't tell you any details, but yes. I am in a bit of a state."

Ben waited for him to continue.

Jason drained his Rum and Ginger. "I've developed a plan which is ethically tricky and may be impossible to implement. Two of my people say I'm crazy and were ready to resign because of my insistence on it."

Jason paused and Ben said, "Go on."

"I have a pretty good track record of getting stuff right. But this time, I'm not sure, and I have a vision of pending doom. That's never happened before. If I insist that we do this, it might make a bad situation even worse."

"And you want my view?"

"Of course."

"Jason, you are a bloody billionaire. You took Avanch and built it to be one of the largest tech companies in the world. I expect you made mistakes, but not that many. This plan you talk about seems like something very big, which is why you're vacillating on it."

Stella delivered a third Heineken to the table and Ben took a swig.

"I believe in you," he continued. "Follow your gut, mate. If you encounter naysayers with other ideas, try talking them around, but if that doesn't work, disregard them. Tell 'em to piss off."

Ben picked up the burger he had ordered and took a bite. Jason looked out over the calm waters of the bay, but his gaze focused on a rainstorm hovering over the nearby Buck Island. He turned to Ben and placed his hand on the man's arm.

Jason leaned forward. "I had a very upsetting dream last night. I can't remember much of it, but there was a lot of blood. It scared the shit out of me."

Ben had been drinking and put his beer back on the table. "Scary. I have those every now and then. But they're usually just dark thoughts that go with the stress. They don't mean anything. Acknowledge them for what they are and move on."

Jason looked away, out over the bay where about twenty yachts hung to their moorings or anchorage. "Ben, are you scared of dying?"

"No point. When it happens, it happens. But if I haven't drunk enough beer that day, I'll feel cheated." He laughed. "Shit, look at me giving you all this sage-like advice. It's probably the booze talking."

Jason smiled and reaching over, giving the gruff Australia a hug. "Thanks. I always appreciate your counsel."

"If I had known that before, I would have ordered the lobster. You are still paying, aren't you?"

Chapter Five

Jack Chen was a renowned chef and owned a highly rated Beijing restaurant. Two weeks before the meeting of the Gang of Four in Baotou, he was approached by an aide from the president's office.

"We are having a very important meeting, and we want you to provide the best of cuisine for the attendees. There will only be eight in total, and the meeting is being held outside Beijing. We'll also need a couple of hundred meals for military and staff."

"Will this be an evening meal? Lunch? Several meals?"

"One day. Snacks on arrival mid-morning, lunch, and perhaps dinner."

The chef was hesitant. The request was an honor, but it would mean closing his restaurant for at least a day and having to tell the customers who had booked tables that he was otherwise engaged. He would need adequate recompense and communicated this to the aide.

"No problem, chef. This meeting seems to be a major event, so cost is not an issue. It is also very secretive. You must not tell anyone what you are doing or where you are going. In fact, we'll fly you there and you won't know the location before you arrive."

Jack asked the question which had been on his mind. "Is the patron for these meals the president?"

The aide looked away. "I cannot tell you that." Jack knew the answer.

He accepted the assignment and then personally called each of the customers who had reservations for the day in question. One of these was Henry Ju-long, a Chinese billionaire, who had once been falsely charged with corruption but had recovered his position in the Chinese hierarchy.

"Mr. Ju-long, I am afraid I have bad news. I have been commanded to cater for another event on the evening you booked with us, and I'll have to close the restaurant on that day. You have been a great supporter for me over the years and I would like to offer you and your lovely wife a complimentary meal on another day of your choice."

"No problem, Jack. But I'm curious. What is this special event?"

Jack Chen hesitated. He didn't know much, and the aide had made it clear that any discussion about it would be classified as treason.

"I can't tell you anything. That was made very clear to me."

"Understood, Jack." Then Henry added as an afterthought, "Remember, I am a friend, not just a customer. Secret events can be risky, and it sounds like you could end up in some sort of trouble with this. If that is so, call me. Friends help one another."

Two weeks later, Jack Chen stood in the kitchen in Yang's air raid shelter, two hundred feet below the ground. He beamed. He was pleased at the way the lunch for the president and his guests had turned out. The kitchen facilities in the bunker were limited, but Jack's innovation and the skills of his staff had overcome these obstacles. He had served a traditional French menu, but had enhanced the dishes with some Chinese accents. The guests were antagonistic with each other, and when the meal was not even finished, he saw President Yang shout at them and they all left to an adjoining conference room.

The identity of the diners did not need guesswork. Their photographs were on newspapers and television news coverage continually, and the languages they used confirmed who they were. His mind went into overdrive.

He was an intelligent and educated man, and knew the world press had no idea that this cabal of leaders was meeting together. Although he was only serving the food, and later snacks and drinks in the conference room, he picked up snippets of the conversations, and speaking with the simultaneous translators, he became aware of details of what was proposed, how it would work, and its name, Global Strike.

He was also aware that little effort had been made to restrict the wait staff, the interpreters, and other administrative individuals from learning the secrets being discussed. The interpreters clearly had a sound understanding of what was being planned. To the chef, it was strange that no security safeguards were in place, and he suddenly reached a realization. None of these people would be leaving the underground bunker alive.

After the meeting concluded and the leaders had departed the facility for their flights back to their homes, Jack supervised the clean-up, but heard the sound of marching feet approaching the kitchen. His people were still in the main dining area clearing away the chairs, and Jack cursed but hid in a cupboard under a sink.

I'm being foolish. Surely there is no real danger here.

Then he heard perhaps twenty soldiers march past his hiding place and into the main area. The sound of their marching boots was followed by the sound of automatic gunfire, which lasted for several minutes. Jack closed his eyes as the realization of what had just happened flooded over him. He knew that all the staff who had knowledge of the meeting were now dead and unable to tell the secrets to their friends or families.

He knew in his heart that he was the only one left with that knowledge, and he might be found at any moment.

Jack waited for two hours in the cupboard and heard the soldiers clearing away the bodies of the staff and interpreters. He felt sorry for the ten people he had brought with him from the restaurant who, no doubt, now lay dead on the floor of the conference room, the kitchen, or elsewhere in the facility.

He heard one of the soldiers talking to another. "Hey. We're one short. There should be twenty-six here and I only counted twenty-five."

Jack stiffened.

"Count again."

"That's difficult. We've already moved some of the bodies to the surface and others are on the way."

"You've just miscounted, idiot. I'm not staying down here for one minute longer than I have to. Have the men move the rest of the bodies up to the trucks and let's close down."

There was more noise as the final bodies were moved, but then the area returned to silence. Jack Chen waited another half hour and peeked out into the kitchen. It was pitch black, and he was sure that the soldiers had cleared the area and turned out the lights. Jack carried a small flashlight, which he had used to examine dishes before they were served, and he used this to find his way to the stairs leading upward. He thought of using the elevator, but reasoned that the sound would be heard and he would be caught. He started up the narrow staircase.

It took him a half hour to negotiate the steep steps, and he was then confronted by a door to the outside, but he found it had been locked.

He was on the edge of despair when he saw another smaller door with a bar. There would be no equivalent mechanism to allow him to return to the space, but that did not matter as he planned to exit the facility and never go back.

It was night, and he observed that most of the troops had departed, but there were three trucks still there with about half a dozen soldiers. The chef crept up to the back of the first truck and peered inside. It was filled with bodies, and as the smell of the already decomposing flesh wafted up, he nearly gagged.

He stepped back, sucked in some fresh air, then slid into the truck among the corpses.

Shortly afterwards, the trucks departed the site and drove to an area in desolate scrub where a bulldozer had already dug a mass grave for the bodies. Jack left the truck before it backed up to the hole, and the soldiers, using garden rakes, pulled the bodies from the truck into the hole.

When their work was complete, the bulldozer filled in the grave and the soldiers returned to the trucks as Jack crept into the back of the third truck.

It was nearly 3:00 a.m. when the convoy drove quietly through the city of Baotou, and no one saw the man who slid out of the slow-moving vehicle and hid in the shadows.

Jack marveled at his escape, but now faced the reality of what to do next. He could not return to his family, nor his restaurant, and then a thought struck him. One of his best customers, who had become a friend over the years, was Henry Ju-long, and he knew that Henry had strong ideas about China's ambitions for the rest of the world. Jack had a smartphone with him and realized that it could be traced, so he retrieved

Henry's number from his contacts and then destroyed the phone.

He found a small breakfast restaurant that catered to haulage workers and those who worked in the nearby quarries and mines. It opened at 4:00 a.m. There, he used the cash he carried with him to warm up and make a call to Henry Ju-long.

He took two days to journey back to Beijing using public buses and walking much of the way, but finally he arrived in the capital and met with Ju-long in a park.

He had not told the billionaire any details, just said the meeting was urgent and needed to be secret. A casual eavesdropper would probably construe the meeting to be about some sexual tryst.

"God, Jack, you look terrible. Are you all right?"

"Mr. Ju-long, I have slept only a little and not eaten for two days."

"Oh, let's go to a restaurant. Get you fed. Your clothes are filthy, too."

"No. Let me tell you what I know first. I'm worried that the authorities may be looking for me. Or even if not, should I turn up, they will know I have escaped."

"Escaped?"

As Jack Chen spewed out his story, Henry shifted from being concerned for the man to being angry at the country's leadership. *Yang is pushing for a world war. Whatever happens, this will end badly for China.*

"Your life is in peril if Yang's goons find out you are still alive." He took out a business card and wrote a telephone number on the back. "Call this number and tell them I sent you. They'll get you out of Beijing to a place of safety."

Henry made up his mind about what to do next, and later that day he called his American friend of many years, Jason Overly.

Chapter Six

During the Baotou meeting, Yang had set out the outline of Global Strike and had called on each of the leaders to commit to the program within a week. Each day, he scanned his communications for confirmation from the Gang of Four as he visualized discussions in each of the other three countries' capitals.

The President of Iran was elected by a vote of franchised Iranians. The Supreme Leader decided the process for this, but in reality, it was he who decided who would be the non-clerical leader of the country.

The Ayatollah had appointed Farid Moradi to the presidency three years earlier, and after the man's return from his meeting in China, the two met. The discussion lasted for several hours.

President Moradi arrived sweating at the office of the Supreme Leader, complaining about the humidity he had driven through in Tehran's late spring. He was delighted by the near freezing temperature that the Ayatollah's staff had set the air conditioning temperature to. He laid out Yang's ideas and the Ayatollah grilled him at length about how the plan would work, who would gain, who would lose, and what risks Iran would take in supporting the audacious approach.

Yang had been clear about the benefits. China would buy large quantities of Iranian oil, which was still sanctioned by most countries. He had also made it clear that if Iran chose not to participate, China would buy its oil from Russia and exclude Iran from its supply channel.

Having offered a carrot and a stick, Yang had gone on to offer other incentives. Russia was already buying drones, and this would be escalated, funded in part by China. In addition, he had agreed with Chekov that Russia would provide hypersonic missile technology and China would lend Chinese nuclear warhead technicians to Iran. These two moves would enable Iran to move rapidly to become a nuclear nation. Iran's uranium enrichment program already provided an "almost" weapons grade product, and with help from Russia and China, they would have what few other countries had: nuclear weaponry.

The president had been looking downwards in deference to the Supreme Leader, but now raised his head. "I suggested to President Yang that we would use this capability to wipe Israel off the face of the earth." The Ayatollah nodded his approval. "When we do this, the threat to other countries in the Middle East will be clear."

Ayatollah Jannali was well known for his hatred of the Jews, as well as Sunni Muslims, and at the end of the meeting, he gave his approval for Moradi to communicate Iran's participation in Global Strike.

Moradi made a call to Yang. "Mr. President, Iran is a 'yes.' "

In Moscow, President Chekov sat in his spacious office in the Kremlin and thought through Yang's plan. Yang had been clear that the details of Global Strike must be shared with no one outside the bunker in Baotou, and Chekov had honored his request.

This was not out of the ordinary for the Russian president, since he normally worked alone to make his decisions and then released them to his allies, his lieutenants, and others in the government and military. Although he always requested their views and critiques of his decisions, everyone knew when asked for their advice, it needed to conform with Chekov's already decided position. No one challenged him, at least not more than once.

He looked around the office and remembered the day when, as deputy prime minister, he had murdered the previous president, Dobry Petrovski, and the prime minister.

They were such idiots, he thought.

His mind shifted back to his current situation and the Chinese president's plan. Chekov's war in Ukraine was not progressing any better than previously, and he was now encountering significant difficulties within Russia. People pointed to his ambitions, which had been unsuccessful and had created more problems than anyone had imagined, even resulting in some attempts at a coup.

If I embrace Global Strike, the heat will be off me. The Americans will cut back their efforts to help Ukraine as they face other challenges across the world.

He noticed that it was starting to rain outside his window when he called Yang. "Mr. President, Russia is in."

In North Korea, Kim was jubilant. He, and his father before him, knew that his actions defying the West and continuing nuclear and missile developments was a game. The United States demanded that he curtail these activities, particularly the test flights, but Kim was able to ignore their demands. However, he also knew that he was in a stalemate position. If he attempted to use his weapons aggressively on the South or on the United States, the response would be rapid and overwhelming. The Americans would destroy him. Now, with allies like China and Russia, he would have a much higher likelihood of success of a re-unification of the two countries under his rule.

He thought about Iran. He was a racist and regarded the Muslims as inferior. Moradi and his Ayatollah worshiped Allah. In North Korea, it was Kim who was God.

His strategic mind thought through the moves and how Global Strike might play out. Yang's initial plan was for Russia to make the first move, quickly followed by Iran. The Ukrainian attack would throw NATO into confusion and the Iranian campaign would lure the West's resources to that theater to protect their oil assets and Israel. If American forces were heavily deployed in the Middle East, his chances in Korea were much greater.

He called Yang to notify the Chinese president of his participation in the plan.

After the call with Kim, Yang's face broke into a broad smile. The Gang of Four was aligned and ready to embark on Global Strike.

Jason's meeting with his friend, Ben, had resulted in a recovery of his confidence that Operation Switch was a valid approach. His nightmare had not recurred, and he had shrugged off the feeling of foreboding that he had felt.

As he was completing his morning swim, an alert sounded on this smartphone, which was on a table near the pool. He swam to the side, picked up the phone, and viewed the message.

The text was short and in bold. "China 1."

Jason frowned. Pulling himself from the pool, he wrapped a nearby towel around him. He dried quickly and descended to his office, closing the door.

He sat behind his desk and accessed his computer. Slipping a Bluetooth headset on, he keyed a few commands into the system.

Henry Ju-long's voice came into his earphones over the encrypted communication.

The Chinese billionaire came straight to the point. "Jason, there are some very dark clouds on the horizon."

"Go on, Henry."

"I am Chinese and proud of it, but President Yang has come up with a plan that will throw my country into chaos and potentially lead to its destruction."

He had known Jason for many years, and knew firsthand of the American's access to clandestine forces. They had never discussed this, but Ju-long assumed that he had strong links with the CIA.

Henry related to Jason what he had learned. "A week ago, there was a major conference here between the heads of China, Russia, Iran, and North Korea. They have described themselves as the Gang of Four and are plotting a massive operation that they are calling Global Strike."

He took a breath and continued.

"Let me tell you." Henry told the tech billionaire how the chef had been present when the plot was being discussed and relayed details of the threat. He did not mention the chef's name.

Henry's narrative was comprehensive, but Jason asked him a few questions to clarify some points.

There was a lull in the conversation as Jason took in the enormity of the situation. The Chinese billionaire then added, "At the end of the meeting, Yang called for them to commit to joining his alliance and they were given one week to confirm this. That would be about now."

"Did your contact think they would accept the plan?"

"He didn't have a take on that. He said there was a lot of suspicion and hostility between the leaders, but Yang can be very persuasive, so my guess is they'll go for it."

"Timing?"

"No indication, but if they decide to do it, they'll need time to prepare, so it'll be a few months off."

Silvia was seated in her Purple Frog office in northern Virginia when she received a call from Jason.

"Hi, Jason," she said as she answered. "I didn't expect to hear from you today. What's up?"

He laid out what he had learned from Henry. Silvia was shocked by the news, but skeptical.

"This might just be a massive fake. Yang may have planted this cook with his story to distract the West."

She visualized her boss shaking his head.

He said, "I want you to check it out."

"What did you have in mind?"

"You're the expert in this stuff. Figure it out, Silvia."

He hung up and Silvia cursed the man.

She summoned Alan to her office and relayed what Jason had told her.

He whistled.

"If it's genuine, this could be the start of World War III," she said.

"Actually, it *would* be World War III."

"We need some verification. We'll start with the planes that visited the Chinese site last week." She called Ching Tong and laid out what she wanted.

An hour later, Ching knocked on her door, and when he entered, he gave her the news.

"As you know, there are various flight tracking sites. From what Henry told us, the chef heard that they all flew in on private executive jets, not their official aircraft. They would be coming from Moscow, Tehran, and Pyongyang. President Yang would also have probably flown there from Beijing."

"Could you track them?" Silvia asked.

"No. I found the likely planes they used and tracked them to the capital cities. Then they turned off their tracking beacons, so if they flew somewhere else—China—there is nothing in the tracking records. The beacons were off for about thirty-six hours, and then they were re-activated and the jets returned to their bases. They might have just been parked, but my bet is that they had their beacons off when they took the flight to and from Baotou."

"Is there any way to check?"

"That's why you have me in Purple Frog. I'm resourceful."

Silvia hid a groan and smiled at the arrogant hacker.

He continued. "I hacked into the sales records for each jet. Each purchased enough fuel to make the trip to Baotou. They probably refueled there for the return trip. That's not conclusive, but it looks like the chef's story checks out."

"The chef said they had military escorts. Can you verify them?"

"No way to check. They don't show up on flight tracking sites."

"The CIA should be able to help. I'll call my buddy, Tina."

Silvia called Tina Graham in Langley. She did not tell the CIA Director about the chef's story, but enquired about possible military flight movements. She gave her dates, times, and flight paths.

An hour later, Tina called Silvia back and shared that the agency had picked up extensive military aircraft traffic into and out of the airport outside Baotou.

Tina sounded frustrated. "Why does Purple Frog want to know about this? It's probably significant, but my people are puzzled and haven't come up with an answer. How you people always seem to know these things before we do has always troubled me."

Silvia decided she needed time to think about the implications and whether she should share information about Global Strike with the CIA.

"I need to think this through, Tina. I'll call you back." She hung up, called Alan into her office, and set up a call with Jason.

Jason loomed large on the videoconference screen. "I believe that the information from Ching and the CIA corroborates the story from Henry. I think we should take this very seriously and plan accordingly."

Silvia nodded her agreement. "I need to tell Tina our findings, but if these four nations follow their plan, I'm not sure what the U.S. can do other than attempt to fight on multiple fronts or sacrifice some of them."

Alan interjected," Yang is a master strategist. He probably sees that the U.S. will opt to engage in just one or two of these battles, and my bet is that he's hoping it will not include China. That way, while one of his allies is being beaten up, he can make his attacks with impunity."

Jason, who had been quiet up until this point, added, "Cut off the heads of the snakes."

Silvia was frustrated by the situation, and Jason's cryptic comment did nothing to relieve her tension. "What do you mean by that?"

"You may not have liked my plan for swapping out Chekov for one of ours, but how about we do all four of these assholes?"

Silvia and Alan lapsed into silence, astounded at the approach their boss was suggesting.

Jason broke the quiet. "This is the most dangerous threat we've ever encountered. I don't want to do this by teleconference. I'll fly up this afternoon and we'll meet tomorrow morning. Okay, Silvia?"

She grunted. "Sure. Why not?"

Chapter Seven

Silvia and Alan both had a love for coffee, but each had different tastes. She liked a drip-feed brew and consumed multiple cups each day, whereas Alan preferred espresso. To her, coffee was something you just poured from the carafe and drank. To him, coffee was a ritual, grinding fresh beans and using the Italian-designed method for a small shot of concentrated caffeine.

Alan had installed a coffee grinder and espresso machine in his office from his first day at Purple Frog, and over the years, he had persuaded Silvia to replicate these in her office and also in the conference room. Silvia matched this with drip-feed machines in all three places.

In was still early morning, but Silvia was drinking her fourth cup as she sat in the conference room with Jason opposite her. Alan was preparing two espressos—one for Jason and one for himself.

Silvia stared at her boss and showed her aggravation. "So let me understand this, Jason. You're suggesting that we assassinate the leaders of China, Russia, Iran, and North Korea along with their deputies. That we replace them with people that Purple Frog controls. And we persuade these replacements to cancel the Global Strike plan. And, we also persuade them to forgo any future military operations outside their own countries. Do I have that right?"

"That's the abbreviated version, but yes, precisely right."

Silvia was aghast." This was a bad enough dream when you only wanted to target Russia, but all four? Russia would have been impossible, but attempting to replicate this scheme three more times is ridiculous."

Alan had been silent until now. He was not known for being loquacious." It probably *is* impossible, but Silvia, can you think of any other way to stop Global Strike? Short of nuking each of them?"

She glared at him. "What are you saying? That you agree with Jason's crackpot idea?"

Jason was starting to feel his patience exhausted and directed a question to Alan. "You and Silvia have labeled the plan impossible, but you're a smart guy. You must be able to come up with a way to pull it off."

Alan shook his head. "Firstly, assassination is not a trivial act. Many years back, the CIA attempted a few operations like this, but they all failed. They haven't tried anything like it for twenty years or more. Well, maybe a minor official or two, but nobody of consequence. Same with MI6. Don't forget, James Bond is a fictional character."

"True," Jason countered, "but the CIA and MI6 have always been hamstrung by bureaucracy, the fear of being caught, and just a lack of secrecy in their operations. If the CIA even discussed something like this, some damn member of Congress would call a public committee and spill it all over the world press. Purple Frog isn't hampered by that sort of thing."

"You know that regime change has always been a no-no for Western countries," Alan said. "I don't think there is anything in writing, but all leaders, in enemy countries as well, avoid assassination attempts on rival leaders."

"So, the President of France may want to take out the Russian president, but doesn't do so because he's scared?" Jason asked. "Scared he'll be taken to the International Criminal Court? Scared the next Russian leader will order a hit on him? Meanwhile, the rest of their populations are the pawns who go to the battlefield and are slaughtered. The West might be worried about the assassination of enemy leaders, but we in Purple Frog are not so constrained."

Silvia poured a fifth cup of coffee. "Interestingly," she said, "if such a scheme was possible, Purple Frog is probably best set up to pull it off. But if we could do what you suggest, it would set us up with dictatorial power. The United States has differentiated itself as a democracy, and the West follows the same model. Our government and leaders are elected by the people, not by some clandestine spy operation from overseas."

Jason snorted. "And we know how well that's working. Most of the West's enemies say they're democratic, but they just pay lip service to the concept. They pretend to be democracies with the population supposedly voting, but in reality, they are autocracies. The leaders we're talking about here are firmly in control and crack down savagely on any moves by the population to disagree with their decisions and actions."

Alan had finished his espresso and set down his cup. "History has shown that sooner or later, the people support a change in power, which often comes violently. Often the military stages a coup and replaces one dictator with one of their own: another dictator. Democracy is not something that comes easily, as we saw with the difficulties that nations faced in the Arab Spring of 2010."

Jason looked at the espresso machine and thought about having another. "One thing is clear: whether the head of state is elected by the voters or if he or she takes power, countries need a strong leader."

Silvia turned to Jason. "So, you're saying that we can morally justify changing dictators? We shall be replacing an electoral vote through our clandestine operations. We shall put new dictators in place."

Jason shook his head. "Or, we could do nothing. We could let Yang and his Global Strike roll out and engulf us in a global war, which will make World War II look like a holiday camp."

Silvia slumped in her chair, exhausted. "If we did this, and we were successful, how would we run it? How would we run the world?"

Jason walked to the espresso machine and looked at it. It was clear he wanted another coffee, but was unsure how the device worked. He enjoyed the strong brew, but being a billionaire, he had never made one himself. Alan took the hint, rose, and started the process as Jason continued his dialogue.

"Our goal is what it has always been. We want to establish world peace, but we'll have to put replacements in power who are not very nice people. They will, no doubt, be brutal with allies of the current leaders, so there will be a lot of bloodletting. We won't interfere and stop them from doing anything internally. But the deal with us will be that they cease external aggression. Russia withdraws from Ukraine, Iran ceases nuclear weaponry development, China recognizes Taiwan, or at least doesn't invade it, and so on."

"What about Global Strike?" Silvia asked, pouring herself another coffee.

"If we implement our plan quickly, the current individuals involved will all be dead and their plan will be inoperable."

"This is not new, is it, Jason?" Alan asked. "You've had this idea for months. Years?"

Jason took the espresso that Alan had handed him. "Actually, from day one of Purple Frog."

Silvia lost it. "You asshole. You played us from the beginning."

"No. On day one, I said we would work to promote a world free of aggressive warfare. We would save lives. Other foundations address health, education, and poverty. We chose to address peace. All the missions you've conducted over the years have been training exercises. Tactical exercises where you have enjoyed great success. You are now ready for the big time."

He stood and looked down at Silvia and Alan.

"Before Global strike, I thought the next step would be against Russia after its criminal attack on Ukraine. Now it's the Gang of Four, and my plan will bring them all down."

The three lapsed into silence.

Alan nodded, indicating that he saw merit in Jason's plan. Silvia shook her head. But, even if they agreed to Operation Switch, they all knew that implementation would be a challenge, and probably not feasible.

Jason broke the silence. "Let's think of this as an exercise for now. I want you to use the froggies to scope out an operation and let's see how feasible it might be."

Sipping her sixth coffee, Silvia raised another issue. "If we want the froggies involved, we'll need to fill them in on what we're considering. I'm not going to tell them it's just a paper exercise. They're going to have their own views on the ethics of the war you are proposing."

Jason drank his coffee. "Agreed. Their insight and positions will be valuable."

Silvia rose to return to her office and turned to the other two. "I need to talk with Tina about Global Strike. The CIA may already be aware of it, but probably not. Between her and the Pentagon, America should be able to come up with an alternative solution. It should be them leading the operation, not us." She looked at her empty coffee cup and the depleted coffee carafe. *I must stop drinking so much coffee,* she thought, *Maybe I'll use a smaller coffee cup?*

When Silvia called Tina Graham at Langley, she did not waste time with trivia.

"Have you heard of something called Global Strike?" she asked.

The CIA director made a sound as if she had been caught off guard. "No. What is it?"

"It's a coordinated attack on the West by four of America's enemies. Four separate operations in four geographies are planned to take place at the same time."

"Coordinated?" Tina asked, sounding surprised. "Four countries?"

"China, Russia, Iran, and North Korea."

Tina gave a short laugh, displaying her disbelief in what Silvia had just told her. "Each one of those countries is a threat, but they don't trust each other, and they even hate each other. There's no evidence they might be working together. I think you've got that wrong."

"I don't think so, but we want you to check it out."

Tina sounded exasperated. *Probably end of a long day,* thought Silvia.

"Okay," Tina said. "Tell me more. What have you got?"

Silvia told her, including all the details that Henry Ju-long had communicated.

She had decided that she would not mention the counter strategy that Jason was pushing. That could wait.

Tina was skeptical. The enormity of the threat was so great that she clearly hoped it was not real.

"What are you basing this on? How did you find out about it? What proof do you have?"

Silvia told her about the Chinese chef and how he had overheard the planning and escaped with his life.

Tina let out a gasp. As she spoke, Silvia visualized a light bulb going off in the CIA director's head. "Shit! So that's what the aircraft were doing in China."

Silvia imagined her shaking.

Tina calmed herself, then spoke. "You seem to know a lot, and if these assholes have found some common ground and a way to work together, the approach makes sense. If they attack at the same time, the West will have difficulty responding." Tina hesitated, then followed up," How certain are you of this? It could be fake. Someone might be selling you a story."

Silvia paused. "That's the reason I'm calling. The CIA has a lot more resources available than we do. Can you check it out? If it's real, there has to be a lot of signs—troop movements, weapon deployment, public statements, the usual stuff."

Silvia heard the CIA director keying information into her computer. She stopped keying, probably reading what she had written, and asked for clarification on a few points.

Tina was silent for a minute, then said, "I agree with you. I'll check it out from our end. If it's real, I'll need to let the president know. We'll need to plan a defense. Hopefully one which will work."

Silvia heard the CIA Director's voice tremble.

"I'll start the investigation immediately. I'll let you know what I find."

She thanked Silvia and hung up.

Silvia sat in her office and looked down at her phone.

I've never heard her like that before. She's scared shitless, she thought.

Chapter Eight

That night, Alan Harlan made a decision. He rarely talked about his job with his wife, Jess. He had never used the name Purple Frog, but Jess had met Silvia a few times and had met many of the froggies at a party after their honeymoon. These meetings had raised more questions than they had answered, but she had not pushed him to find out more.

She knew the basics. He worked for a spy agency, which was not a governmental organization, but targeted "bad guys." She did not know much more.

With the current threat and possible countermeasure, Alan needed her involved. He knew at a certain time, he would have to decide whether he supported Jason's plan. He needed her advice, and he needed her buy-in.

He smiled when he thought about how excited and aroused she became when he hinted at some of his activities. His "James Bond" persona turned her on, and soon after he'd told her about the bare bones of some missions he had been involved in, they had made love.

Tonight was going to be different. Tonight, he would tell her everything. He had not discussed this with Silvia or Jason, but the imminent threat from the Gang of Four and Purple Frog's possible response were too important to leave her out.

He sat in their living room and nursed his Scotch. He glanced over at her as she texted her friends, reading their replies and sipping her Chardonnay.

He leaned forward. "Darling, there's something important that I want to talk to you about." His demeanor was serious, and she gave him a short laugh, thinking it was a joke.

She looked up, recognized his facial expression, frowned, and put down her phone. "That doesn't sound good."

He put down his Scotch. "You know I work for a clandestine operation." He paused. "Well, something big has come up."

He hesitated again and she asked him, "And you want to tell me about it?"

"Yes."

"Are you off somewhere? Is it dangerous?"

"No. It's more than that."

She started to show alarm. "Are you in trouble? Are we in trouble?"

"It's an external threat from our country's enemies that could result in a major conflict."

She stared at him, waiting for him to continue. He did so.

"If the threat is real, it will mean a third world war. A war that would be far more devastating than the other two. It could result in the total destruction of the earth."

"Alan, you're scaring me."

"I know. I'm sorry. But you need to know. Normally I wouldn't get you involved, but this time, you need to understand what's happening and I want your input on a possible solution we're considering. Obviously, this is top secret, and you can't talk about this with anyone else."

"Of course. I understand."

Alan told her about the Gang of Four and Global Strike and she turned pale. Jess was an accomplished AI programmer for a military contractor, and she had become knowledgeable about modern warfare systems.

"Is it real? Are you sure this is not some game being played on you? Conspiracy theory? Fake news?"

"I'm not sure, but we have the CIA running a check and should hear from them tomorrow. My gut feeling, though, is that it's real."

She looked about their apartment, then back at her husband. "How can we confront something like that? Even with the military resources of the U.S., NATO, and a few other allied countries, fighting this war on four fronts will be impossible. I'm not a military strategist, but the conclusion is obvious." She shook her head. "I know you don't work for the CIA or MI6 or any of the government spy agencies, but what are they doing about it?"

"They've only just found out about it. In fact, my people discovered the plot, and this afternoon, my boss called our CIA contact."

"So, they'll handle it."

"Hopefully."

"But your organization has another plan?"

"You know me so well, Jess Harlan."

He explained Operation Switch and Jess's eyes widened.

"If you do that and pull it off, it might well work. But it'll put Jason, Silvia, and you in an incredible position of power. You'll call the shots for every rogue nation. I guess Jason will be running the show, and he did run a huge corporation, but even so." Her voice trailed off as she processed the enormity of the Purple Frog plan.

She stood and started pacing about their living room.

"You say that Jason put this plan together twelve years ago without telling you?"

"Yes. It's been always there, and we didn't see it."

Jess stared at her husband. "Can you trust him? He'll be playing God. Can he handle it?"

"I don't know. They say that absolute power corrupts absolutely."

Alan grew silent as Jess asked," Are you in favor of the plan?"

Alan did not answer her question. "It's a long shot. Pulling it off in one country would be nearly impossible, but doing it successfully in four?"

"Can I help?"

"I need you as an independent sounding board. Silvia is opposed to the plan, and the Advisory Board may also be opposed."

"And you? Do you support it?"

"I'm not sure, but if we can come up with a way to implement, I'm inclined to go for it."

"The way you describe it, it sounds like it's all about assassinating four country presidents and probably their number twos. Are you really telling me that? Is Alan Harlan going to become a murderer? Are you going to get a gun and go and shoot them? I can't believe you're saying that."

"You already know something about our organization, and you know we use some very unorthodox methods. I think it's time I told you the full story. You may hate me when I'm done, but it's time you knew everything."

They talked for an hour as Alan gave Jess the details of Purple Frog's operations.

"My God, Alan. This is a lot to take in." Jess sat back, her mind swimming. "But, you seem to have the resources and can pull off this Operation Switch, if anyone can." Then, as an afterthought, she asked, "Silly question, but why did you call the organization, 'Purple Frog'?"

Alan laughed. "Google it. A purple frog exists and is a shadowy creature. It lives underground and only emerges once a year for a specific action, then returns to hiding. A purple frog's safety requires it to stay hidden, under the radar."

She gave him a grin." I'll bet the specific action is sex."

Alan nodded. She reached over and kissed him.

Jess asked a lot of questions which Alan answered. He became silent as did she.

Jess reached out and they kissed again. "Thanks for telling me all this. Thanks for trusting me enough. I knew it was something like that, but I also knew I couldn't push you for the whole story. I love you and I trust you. Oh, there were times when I had my doubts. Remember when you were coping with that white supremacist? But I soon got over that."

He stared at her. "So, what do you think I should do about Operation Switch?"

"If you want to do this, I'll support you. One hundred percent. But with something like this, you can't be wishy-washy about it. You need to make your decision and then stay the course."

"And if I decide not to support the plan?"

"If Jason keeps pushing it and you can't support the idea, resign. I make good money and we have savings. You'll find another job in no time. We'll be fine."

"I love you so much. I didn't want to trouble you, but we are in this together. I guess it's been preying on my mind."

Jess dropped her head onto his shoulder. "I could tell. Last night you were obviously having a nightmare and thrashing about like you were in a fight."

Alan glanced at her again. "I remember it vaguely. No details. But there was a lot of blood, or something like it."

Yang had three generals working with him on the program, and they jointly decided on the attack schedule. He had insisted that China would be last to strike so that if the others failed for some reason, he would be able to reconsider and re-maneuver to avoid a Chinese catastrophe.

There was a lot of preparatory work to be done in each country, and Yang called for each of the leaders to develop and present their detailed set of actions, particularly for the initial offensive. He and his generals received their plans and built them together into a cohesive directive.

They were conscious that, although time was needed to prepare their actions, every day spent before the launch was another day when some details of Global Strike might leak out.

Over the next month, Yang was busy, as were each of the other leaders on their battle plans, assessing the resources and time scale for a rapid implementation.

He spoke with each one individually every few days. Each leader was experienced and smart. Each knew, even as they developed detailed plans, something would disrupt the endeavor. A German field marshal in 1871 had written an essay reaching the conclusion that *"No plan survives first contact with the enemy."* Regardless, the plans were developed, and it was time for the Gang of Four to meet together.

Yang called an encrypted videoconference with the other three leaders.

"Fellow leaders," he said, "we have individually discussed and debated your battle plans, and it is now time to agree on them and start the implementation. We have debated these for weeks now, and it's time to pull the trigger."

He paused, looked into the camera, and smiled.

"Based on what you have sent us, we should start the attacks in late February, next year."

The countdown to *Global Strike* had started.

Silvia heard the shrill noise of the smartphone dedicated to calls with the CIA director. She reached over and answered.

"Hi, Tina," she said.

"Hi."

The CIA director sounded agitated.

"You sound upset," Silvia said.

"You're right, and that's why I called. I've had our people check out your story about Global Strike, and there are a lot of indications that it's valid. Firstly, in China, there is an increase in troop movements and a buildup or military hardware close to Taiwan. It's more than usual and more than just a drill."

Silvia asked, "South China Sea?"

"They seem to be consolidating. No real movement, but they seem to be readying for a defensive battle."

"The other countries?"

Silvia heard Tina riffling through her notes before speaking. "In North Korea, there's been mobilization as well, and deployment of short-range missiles to firing points close to the DMZ. Even worse, several ICBMs are being prepared. Russia is quiet, but we've noticed that they've recently avoided their usual propaganda threats about the use of nuclear weapons. Iran just announced that their revenge against Israel is imminent."

Tina again riffled through her notes.

"We also tracked a shipment of long-range missiles from Russia to Iran, and they are probably being installed there. We know Iran has developed and stockpiled weapons-grade uranium, but we don't have any intel about their ability to create a nuclear warhead."

Tina took a deep breath, then continued.

"We've reached out to the diplomats. The ambassadors to the U.S. for China, Russia, and Iran seem at a loss regarding the current foreign policy for each of their countries. Each one believes something big is about to go down, but they have not been brought into the loop. They're not happy."

"North Korea?"

"We have an asset in the North Korean mission to the United Nations, but he hasn't heard anything either. The presidents are keeping things very close to their chests."

Tina paused and Silvia guessed what she would say next.

"The intel is not definitive, but supports the theory that Global Strike is real and imminent."

Silvia exhaled. "Do you have a plan to counter something like this?"

Tina was silent for twenty seconds and then said, "No. Nothing in the CIA. But this is a Pentagon matter. I'll work with them to figure something out, but before doing that, I need to brief the president."

Chapter Nine

From the first day, twelve years before, when the Purple Frog team started its operations, it was clear that it would face some situations where the means did not justify the ends. To address this, they established an Advisory Board, and each mission that skirted or broke legal constraints was referred to this body for review. The Board had been set up when Jason was still running Avanch, and had little day-to-day involvement in the clandestine agency. The Board comprised Jason and two others.

Matthew Brown was an African American now in his mid-seventies. For nearly fifteen years, he had worked in a Washington think tank that addressed global issues of cyber warfare, economy, climate change, and political infrastructure, but he had recently retired. When the organization was starting up, he'd partnered with Jason to formulate the charter for Purple Frog and had served on the Board since then.

Soon after Purple Frog was up and running, Alice Gronon, a superior court judge in her fifties, joined him and brought a rich understanding of international law and views on justice. At first, she had been appalled that, to achieve its objectives, Purple Frog on many occasions violated the law, but she was a pragmatist and reasoned that it was more important that justice was served even when outside the laws, which were often implemented for political purposes. One of her strengths was in her evaluation of missions that would involve harm to America's enemies, and in some cases their assassination. She was careful in her assessment of each of these, and while not prohibiting unorthodox and illegal acts, she brought her judgment to review these actions. Over the years she'd shifted to a belief that, in many circumstances, the ends did justify the means.

Jason and the two worked with Silvia and her management team reviewing operations and offering guidance. As Matthew explained in the early days, the Advisory Board was just that—advisory. They offered advice, but did not make decisions. Matthew also cautioned that if their advice was ignored too often, they would resign.

Jason called a video conference with the other two Board members. Silvia and Alan joined the call. He laid out the intel on the Gang of Four, Global Strike, the CIA's confirmation of the plot, and his plan for Operation Switch.

At first, he was greeted by disbelief. Matthew held off from the conversation as he thought through the ramifications. Alice, however, showed her disagreement immediately.

"Jason, I accept the dangers of Global Strike, but you're advocating the assassination of four world leaders, and then setting up a Star Chamber from which you will rule the world."

He had expected this to be her reaction, but kept calm. He looked her in the eyes. "I believe there are three areas to discuss. Firstly, how real is the Global Strike threat? Secondly, can we morally justify Operation Switch? And thirdly, if we decide to do it, how likely are we to be able to implement?"

Matthew spoke for the first time. "Tell me more about this Global Strike."

Jason laid out all that they knew, including what Silvia had learned from her conversation with Tina.

Alice threw her head back. "But it may not be real."

"The CIA has concluded that it probably is," Silvia said.

"Does the CIA have an answer to the threat?" the judge asked.

"No," Silvia replied. "They don't have one yet, but the director is meeting with the president and we'll see where that takes them."

Alice snorted. "Why are we even discussing this? It's up to the U.S. government to address this issue. This is not a Purple Frog problem."

"I agree," Jason answered. "This is something that the government should be addressing, but what if they can't find a solution? Operation Switch offers a backup plan. Hopefully, we won't need to implement it, but if we do, we'll need to move fast. I want to have agreement on it, in case we need to act."

Alice sighed in exasperation. "Whatever happened to democracy, Jason? What you are advocating is an autocracy with you at its head. That's not the American way. Our system doesn't work perfectly, but we have a constitution that may be centuries old, but it is still a sound basis for governance."

She was not wearing her judge's robe, but everyone on the call imagined her doing so as she continued.

"I want to make one thing clear: we don't go out assassinating leaders we don't like and blackmailing others to allow us to rule the world. I've had my concerns about the activities of Purple Frog over the years, but have come to terms with them. This, however, is a step too far."

Jason sighed. "Alice, this is just a logical extension of what we have always done. Yes, we break the law, but our successes have come because of that.

Our past missions have been incredibly important, but they've been short-term, tactical, and limited. What we have here is a strategic approach, which, when we pull it off, will allow an order of magnitude reduction in global hostilities." Jason noticed that Matthew Brown was leaning forward, waiting for an opening, but he finished his monologue. "Operation Switch will prevent a world war."

"This is a shock, Jason," Matthew said, entering the discussion. "I accept that Operation Switch is an extension of what the Frog has been doing for over a decade, but it is such a huge extension."

Jason turned his attention to Alice. "You talk about democracy, but the people we are dealing with don't believe in it anyway. Yang, Chekov, Moradi, Kim. All they want is autocracy and to extend their power beyond their borders. We are not taking a gun to a knife fight. They are already toting."

"If we do this," Matthew asked, "won't our enemies then target our president? The UK prime minister? The head of the EU?"

"You don't think they have plans for that, already?" Alan asked.

Matthew nodded. "You're right. And if you can get away with this operation, it'll save thousands of lives. Poor kids who will be conscripted and sent off to war to die."

The others on the conference link waited for him to continue.

"However, even if we agree to the principle, how are you going to pull it off? You've said yourself that you need to assassinate these people and get specific replacements in place. Then you have to use some sort of leverage to force the replacements to do what you want. I can just about go with the concept, but practically, it's impossible."

Alice added, "I just can't go along with the ethical aspects. We should not be doing something like this, even if we could implement it successfully."

Jason sighed with impatience. "Global Strike will bring about World War III. Is that what you want? Like it or not, Operation Switch has the best chance of preventing that."

Matthew grimaced. "I'm not happy about it, but it looks like an acceptable option. Hopefully, the Pentagon or CIA come up with a better alternative. If not, I support the approach."

Alice said quietly, "I'm still opposed."

Jason let out a sigh. Silvia was silent, as was Alan.

As they were wrapping up, the judge raised a point." If you did implement Operation Switch, who will manage the control of the replacements over the longer term?"

Jason looked at her. "That will be me and my team at Purple Frog."

She sniggered. "Jason Overly, previous CEO at Avanch and now Emperor." As an afterthought, she added," With our largest enemies in your control, you should probably be called 'Galactic Emperor.' "

After the call with the Advisory Board, Silvia walked to the side table in her office and poured a cup of coffee. She had switched to decaf, and when she took a sip, she screwed up her face. *I need the real thing.*

She sat at her desk and looked at Alan, who was opposite her. "I'm still having problems with this," she said. "I can't get my head around the implications, even if we can pull it off."

He watched her trying to think through the issue, but his mind returned to a few evenings before with Jess. She was so right in her advice, and he had concluded that he would support Jason's operation. A smile spread over his face as he recalled their lovemaking afterward.

He turned to Silvia. "I can see where you're coming from. But with Global Strike on the horizon, I can't think of a better plan."

Silvia came close to throwing the insipid coffee against her wall, but restrained herself. "So, Jason becomes Galactic Emperor? He runs the world. From his palace in St. Croix. Then one day, he has a hangover, or something else upsets him. He is swindled by some scam company. So, he pushes the Russian leader to launch an attack on the company. If he can't get his way about something, does he order one of our puppets to launch a nuclear strike?"

"Silvia, we discussed this. The three of us will be involved in decisions, just as we are now. He can be pigheaded, but he's not stupid. And we'll use the Advisory Board to help."

Silvia shook her head. "If he runs the show, what does that make me?"

"I guess 'Galactic Princess' would be a good title."

That evening, Alan brought Jess up to date on his meetings with the Advisory Board and later with Silvia.

She was incredulous." 'Galactic Princess'? Are you losing it, Alan?" She laughed." You're calling your boss 'Galactic Princess'?"

He shrugged. It was a stupid title.

She snuggled up to him. "But seriously, you seem to have made your mind up to support the operation."

"You're right. But I'm still hoping that the CIA and Pentagon can come up with an alternative. It shouldn't be up to Purple Frog to face this attack alone."

"Jess nodded. "In my work, I've seen a lot of senior people from various branches of the military and government. They are all bright people and have the right ideas, but politics always comes into the picture, and they make decisions which make no sense, just to reinforce their territories or to make a point."

Alan stood and refreshed Jess's wine and his Talisker. "That's one of the joys of Purple Frog. Oh, we have our disagreements, but, being small, we can address them rapidly, agree on a path forward, and get on with it."

Jess sipped her Chardonnay." My bet is that trying to address Global Strike will cause a turf war in the U.S. military and they'll be slow to react. That could be disastrous. They'll see the answer as needing huge numbers of troops and major hardware. Even if we are successful, that will lead to untold destruction. And they'll assume that significant troop casualties are a cost of war and accept that. Operation Switch, as you've described it, will result in few—if any—casualties other than the targeted presidents."

Alan sipped his Scotch. "Tina needs the president on her side so she can head off some of the disputes. As I've told you, she's a no-nonsense woman, and if she can take the lead on this, we stand a much better chance of success. She has a meeting set up for the end of the week."

Chapter Ten

Jason had returned to his Caribbean Island home and sat on his deck looking out over the pool. The weather was warm, with a light breeze, and the only sound was the distant lapping of waves on the beach below. Ordinarily, it would be a time to relax, enjoy a cold drink, and look forward to a dinner that Doris would prepare for him. But today, his mind was racing as he thought about the operation to replace four leaders of enemy countries.

The intercom from the gate below rang and he frowned. He was not expecting anyone, and Doris ran over and answered it.

A male voice echoed out of the intercom. "Hi, it's David. I have the fresh herbs you wanted."

Jason looked at her." Who's David?"

"Our neighbor. He's retired and grows terrific herbs. I called him this morning, since we are running short and I need them for a special dinner tonight."

Jason had not met David, but knew his property. His mind shifted to consider his own safety. *Does the man work for the Gang of Four? Have they discovered that Purple Frog and I are aware of Global Strike? Has this David been tasked with silencing me? Am I being paranoid?*

He remembered a time that coincided with the birth of Purple Frog when he'd suffered from paranoia and had instituted a series of investigations of key managers in his technology company. His fears had proven groundless, and he'd suffered anxiety as an aftereffect. It was during this time that he had developed the bare bones of Operation Switch, but had decided not to share it with Silvia and Alan. *Is my overall judgment suspect?*

He now experienced a bolt of fear that Switch would be a disaster. *Maybe this plan of mine is flawed. Maybe it'll result in a worse situation than we have today.*

His mind returned to the present, thought of his mysterious neighbor, and instructed Doris. "Wash the herbs thoroughly, Doris. Use boiling water."

"Jason, don't you be silly, now. That would ruin them. David doesn't use pesticides, and they were cut just this morning. You leave this to me."

Jason shook his head. *Paranoia again?* he wondered.

She cocked her head to one side, asking for Jason's approval to let the man in. He nodded and she activated the remote gate at the end of the long driveway.

Jason's phone rang and he saw the call was from Silvia, so he left Doris and descended to his office.

"Hi, Jason," she said when he answered. "It's Silvia, and I have Alan with me."

"Hi, Silvia. What's up?"

"Tina is meeting with the president today before briefing the Pentagon. Alan and I have done a lot of soul-searching about Operation Switch, and if we need to implement it, he's a supporter. I am not."

Jason picked up a pen from his desk and clicked the point out and then back in a few times. "It seems we're split on this. You know I'm for it and so is Matthew. Alice is opposed. And making it happen may still be impossible."

"Whatever way this goes down, there'll be a lot of blood spilled."

As she said this, Jason's mind went to his dream and his recent meeting with Ben.

"Jason, are you still there?" Silvia's voice broke through his thoughts.

He shook his head and said, "The Pentagon may not be successful, so we need a backup. Find a way to make Switch work. As a *backup*," he reiterated.

"All right," Alan said, answering for them.

Jason hung up.

Jason Overly, while building and managing his technology firm for two decades, had experienced his share of trauma.

The public reads about the industry giants and imagined their lives, enjoying expensive meals, staying at the best hotels, and flying in private jets. They often overlooked how executives put in long hours of hard work each day, faced the stress of dealing with Wall Street, banks, shareholders, the media, government, and rivals, not to mention the political and personality conflicts which occur within any organization.

While CEO at Avanch, he'd had few days, even on weekend, that he could go to a golf course or have a long lunch with friends. Retirement had changed that, and he was loving it. *If only you were here with me, Sarah,* he thought as images of his deceased wife, the love of his life, flashed through his head.

One trait he had found useful over the years in combatting stress was to force himself to take a minimum of an hour or two each day to forget the day-to-day traumas and enjoy a good evening meal with a couple of drinks. Global Strike and Operation Switch had consumed him for the past few weeks, but now, he sat at his dining table and Doris presented him with a small roasted leg of lamb, allowing him to carve however much he wanted. It smelled delicious. Separately, she provided roasted potatoes, grilled local zucchini, and a rich gravy.

"This is local lamb, and the herbs are rosemary and marjoram. Courtesy of David," Doris said.

Jason carved himself thick slices of the lamb and poured some gravy onto it. Doris had cooked it medium rare. He tasted it and the flavors of the rosemary and marjoram filled his mouth and mind. The billionaire relaxed.

"Doris, this is delicious. Thank you. Oh, and please thank David when you see him."

"Will do. He'll be so happy. I've known him for years now, and he and his wife are lovely people."

Jason's eyes roamed the table and focused on the lamb. Where he had carved, a little blood escaped and trickled onto the platter. His dream flashed back into his mind.

"To hell with that," he said aloud and poured himself another glass of the Bordeaux Doris had decanted to accompany the meal.

I wonder how Tina Graham's meeting with the president went?

———⚭———

Bill Draper, President of the United States of America, sat at the Resolute Desk and frowned. The world around him was becoming more dangerous, and many of America's enemies were growing their armed forces and weaponry. They were also making more statements with implied threats to the West.

Worse still, his poll ratings were in free fall.

My second term is coming up and I need to concentrate my attention on winning the election, he thought. *Key to re-election is downplaying global conflict.*

His personal assistant announced that the CIA Director had arrived for a requested meeting and was waiting.

Damn, I forgot about that. She probably has some bad news or some catastrophe she wants me to address.

"Good morning, Tina," he said as she entered, faking a broad smile.

"Good morning, Mr. President." Tina came straight to the point. "Sir, we have credible evidence of a major threat that will shortly face the United States."

Damn woman. "Tell me the bad news."

She did so.

The president turned ashen and slumped back in his chair.

"This is serious stuff. Are you sure of your facts?"

"We're not certain, but if this Chinese chef is to be believed, the threat is real."

"A bloody cook. What if he's a fake? What if he's just stupid and angling for some U.S. dollars? What if Yang is playing with us? Just another bit of disinformation."

"That's possible, sir. But unlikely."

"Where did you get this story, anyway? Your agents in China?"

Tina feared this line of questioning. "No. It came from Purple Frog."

"That damned secret operation you work with? What is the U.S. getting from all the billions we spend on the CIA when everything appears to be accomplished through this Purple Frog?"

He swiveled on his chair and faced away from her, looking out his window onto Pennsylvania Avenue.

"This whole thing sounds fishy to me. Yang working with Chekov? That I can understand and accept, but all four of these countries working together is unlikely. They all hate each other."

"I agree, sir, but our own tracking places aircraft from each country converging on the city in China where Purple Frog says the meeting and the initial planning took place. I've instituted a significant further investigation and our conclusion is clear. Global Strike is real."

"Tell me more about your investigation, Director."

She did so and concluded, "My people believe it's credible, and I believe we must treat it as such. I'll set up a briefing session with the Pentagon and see what they recommend as a countermeasure."

"You'll do no such thing. If you do, the media will find out about it and tell it to the world. I have an election coming up, and something like this could be a death blow. It would indicate that I've allowed this to happen on my watch. Everyone will say it's my fault."

Tina Graham sat silently, waiting for the president to calm down and address the issue.

He rose and started pacing. "It may not be imminent, or it may not even be real, so I'm not going to mess up my re-election chances. Let me have a report and I'll discuss with the NSA."

"Mr. President, this matter is urgent."

"Tina, Tina, Tina. Everything is urgent. But I have more pressing issues at the moment. Get me a report by the end of the month."

Tina gasped.

"Until then, this discussion stays between you and me," he said. "Keep your eyes open, but don't alert anybody else. Even in your agency. This Global

Strike will probably blow over and I can address it in my second term, if I need to."

Tina was stunned. "Sir, with respect, that's an irresponsible line to take."

"Don't you talk to me like that."

"I'm sorry, sir, but this is important—"

"I've made up my mind. Not a word of this matter outside this office. Do I make myself clear?"

"Mr. President, I cannot go along with that."

"Then resign, Director. And remember, if you leak this, I'll have your…" He was about to say "balls," but realized the term was inappropriate.

It was clear that the meeting was over, and Tina rose unsteadily and departed the Oval Office.

Tina was incensed and on her return trip to Langley, pondered what she should do about it. On entering her office, she opened her computer and wrote a letter of resignation. She printed it, signed the document, and was about to place it in an envelope when she stopped herself.

She was certain that Global Strike was real, and if the president was not prepared to act on it, perhaps Purple Frog could gather further intel to change his mind. If she resigned, her replacement was unlikely to pursue the matter, and this might lead to doing nothing until the strike was launched. It could mean the destruction of the United States. Better she remain in her position and pay lip service to the president's request to keep quiet.

I need to talk with Purple Frog, she thought.

"Hello, Tina." Silvia said, answering the call and placing her phone on speaker so that Alan, who was in her office at the time, could hear the dialogue.

The CIA director's voice quaked as she told Silvia about her interchange with the president.

Silvia was shocked at the president's stand. "That's terrible. We both believe the threat is real, and your CIA intel confirms it. If the Pentagon is blindsided on this, the result will be catastrophic. What the hell is the president thinking?"

"He's fixated on being re-elected, and releasing this could damage his chances."

"So, he's sticking his head in the sand?"

"That's exactly what he's doing. Initially, I decided to resign, but I've since reconsidered. I even considered going public with the story, but that would be regarded as a political ploy, or worse, and I'd end up in a prison cell somewhere. In the end, I decided that I can do more if I remain in place."

Silvia put her coffee cup down. "We were expecting, and hoping, you could work with the Pentagon and come up with viable countermeasures, but obviously that's not going to happen now."

The CIA director sighed. "Frankly, even if the president wanted us to put together a plan, I'm not sure we could come up with anything that would work."

Silvia paused. "Actually, we have a plan which is evolving. It might address the issue. It would have been better for you to handle the problem, but that's obviously not going to happen."

Tina gasped. "Really? Purple Frog can solve this one? You people amaze me. How are you going to do it?"

"We're still in an early stage. At this time, I don't want to share."

Silvia reflected a moment on Operation Switch.

"Actually, it's probably better that you don't know." Silvia nodded to Alan and then added, "It's a good idea that you stay with the agency. What we are planning will likely require access to a lot of additional intel about each of the four countries and their leaders. It would be very helpful to be able to access CIA resources."

"Okay. Anything we can do, we shall."

Silvia terminated the call.

Chapter Eleven

Alan spoke first. "Holy shit."

Silvia swiveled around on her chair. "'Holy shit' sums it up."

"So, I guess it's up to us."

"I guess so."

"And we'll implement Jason's pet project."

"I guess so."

"Holy shit."

She glanced at him. "Can you do it?"

"I've already had people considering options, but there have not been any magical solutions yet. However, I'll get it done. Not sure how, but we're a resourceful lot. I'll set up some teams to address each country separately."

Silvia shook her head. "I still don't like it, but I can't see another option. Let's call Jason. He'll try hard not to gloat."

She gave Alan a small smile and reached for her phone.

Five minutes later, she had brought her boss up to date. When she described the president's stance on the threat, she heard his heavy breathing on the line. "Damned politicians," was all he said. He seemed to hesitate as he thought through the situation. "So, we're stuck with Switch. Like it or not."

Silvia sighed. "Yes. That's my conclusion as well."

"Can we pull it off?" he asked.

"Alan has some ideas and will be setting up some froggie task forces to come up with plans. I haven't told Tina about Switch, but I said we needed help from CIA resources. She agreed."

Jason grunted. "We are embarking on a journey, and must be successful or we shall be in a world war. I'll talk to the Board. Otherwise, let me know how I can help."

In St. Croix, Jason Overly finished his call with Silvia and gave a short laugh. He did not feel the elation he had expected. *I hope Alan can pull it off.*

From the first discussion of Operation Switch, Alan had undertaken a lot of the preparatory work developing plans in case they were needed. While Silvia had authorized the work despite her concerns about the overall morality and ethics of the plan, Alan had a few ideas already and had sketched out the structure for four task forces, one for each country.

Although she had not said it out loud, Silvia figured that if the operation was impossible to implement, Jason would back off and Purple Frog could return to normal. *Well,* she thought, *with Global Strike hovering above our heads, not really normal.*

Now the world had changed. Its future probably depended on Purple Frog's success with Operation Switch.

———❈———

Silvia called an all-hands meeting and explained Global Strike and the countermeasures that Jason had formulated. She concluded by telling them about the reaction of the U.S. President.

"The CIA is convinced that the threat is real, but with the president's directive, the U.S. is not even starting to address a way to combat it. Before this turn of events, Alan and I had not fully made up our minds about Operation Switch, but that decision has now been decided for us. Unless one of you can come up with a better plan, we are going full steam ahead."

She paused a moment, then continued.

"I'm sure you'll face the same internal thoughts about the ethics of what we are proposing, and I want to hear from each of you if you don't want to be a part of it."

She looked around at the stunned faces of the froggies.

"As usual, you can communicate with Alan or me in whatever way you want. Face-to-face meetings, email exchanges, and even texts. If you want to remain anonymous, that's okay. Put your comments through HR and Helen and her assistant will ensure we see them but without attribution."

Silvia asked for initial questions and sensed that everyone understood the enormity of the endeavor. She decided to address this.

"If we can come up with a way to implement this operation, it is going to dwarf every other operation that we've undertaken in Purple Frog. Be assured we are not taking this lightly."

Alan took over. "My priority now is to determine how to do it. How do we eliminate the heads of the Gang of Four, how do we identify and compromise replacements, and how do we ensure that the new leaders implement our 'no war/no aggression' agenda?"

He keyed a few commands into his laptop and the large screens around Purple Frog's offices were filled with an organization chart.

"I've set up four task forces, one for each country. Each has a mix of froggies. Each has two profilers, a translator fluent in the country's language, one person from money laundering, one from Ching Tong's hackers, and one from Donna's field operations. Since they know the leaders best, a profiler will head up each team. Vivienne La Croix, Russia, Liz Howard, Iran, Too Min, North Korea, and Ken Lin, China."

He scrolled through charts that laid out the members of each country's team.

"I'm going to meet with each team separately and we'll work through what needs to be done. Operation Switch is all about replacing the leaders in these countries with ones that we control. Use your expertise and imagination. Profilers, one of your first steps will be to identify who we need to remove."

Liz Howard, who specialized in Iran, said, "So, for Iran, we replace the Supreme Leader and the president?"

Alan nodded. "You would know that better than I. You also have to come up with replacements. Start with a list and then narrow it down. I'm looking for a strong set of arguments for who you believe the best candidate is."

"Do you want us to address how we can compromise the replacement?" Liz asked.

"Absolutely. Use the money laundering and hacker members as appropriate. The replacement will, no doubt, face threats from rivals or allies of the former president, so we need to find ways of neutralizing these. I don't want us involved, but we might be required to help out."

Alan consulted some notes on his laptop.

"Donna's people will work on the best way to remove the current leaders," he continued. "I prefer accidental deaths, but these people are very well protected, so I'll settle for whatever is most effective."

Donna and her people nodded their acceptance of their role and Kemal, one of her field operations team, added, "Will you want a plan to keep the replacements in line when they assume power?"

"Yes."

The room was silent.

"Any questions?" No one spoke and Alan concluded," We have ambitious goals, and I want bold plans to achieve them. Silvia, Jason, and I have done a lot of soul-searching about Operation Switch. I'll repeat what Silvia said. We hadn't decided to take this path until we found out about the president's stance on the matter. Now, we have no choice. Ladies, gentlemen, the future of the Western world is in your hands. We are going to do the impossible. Go get me answers."

Two weeks later, Alan and Silvia met the Iranian task force to discuss the plan for that country. The team made a brief but well-supported presentation. Liz Howard's knowledge of Iran and the key players was the best Purple Frog had, and she had been the logical choice to lead the team.

Silvia knew many of the answers already, but wanted to test the team's understanding of the situation and their recommendations. She asked, "Who comprises the entrenched power at present, Liz?"

Liz Howard had a habit of rambling, but after being counseled on this trait previously, she'd resolved to be short and direct in her answers. "Ayatollah Mohammad Jannali and the president, Farid Moradi."

"Jannali is the Ayatollah?" Alan asked.

"He's one of them. Ayatollah is a title for a senior cleric. There are about a hundred of them, and many are members of the Assembly of Experts. They decide who among them is named Supreme Leader. If we can remove the current Leader, the next in line for the role will be appointed by the Assembly of Experts."

"Will they appoint our candidate?"

"It's unlikely that he'll be their first option. The most likely choice will be as bad as the one we'll be replacing."

"Can we just work on the presidential post? Bypass the Supreme Leader?"

"The president is allegedly elected by the voters, but in reality, the Ayatollah appoints him. Under the next Ayatollah, the president is likely to be the current head of the Quds. And we certainly don't want him."

"So, I assume you have a way of making this work."

"I recommend we focus on the top position. The Supreme Leader has the ultimate power, and General Rahimi, head of the Quds, may try to influence him, but would not have the power to remove him or even override whatever he wants to do."

Alan nodded his agreement. "So who do we want, then?"

Liz smiled. "Ahmad Kani. He is a well-respected cleric and is a moderate." She consulted a file she had brought with her. "Privately, he has deplored the aggressive stance that the current Supreme Leader has taken and believes that Islam is a peaceful religion. He doesn't advocate the destruction of Israel nor the extension of Iran's sovereignty."

Silvia sipped her coffee. "How can we get him into the top position?"

"We eliminate the first choice."

"Assassination? A third assassination?"

"No. Compromise. Despite the man's clerical credentials, the number one candidate is rumored to have had his first wife raped and murdered. There is little evidence available, but we could build up a public outcry against him when we are ready to replace the current leader. The threat of exposure might be enough to have him stand down."

Silvia put her coffee cup down. "Did he really kill his wife?"

Liz shrugged. "Probably."

Alan keyed some notes into his laptop. "Let's assume that will work and Kani becomes the new Supreme Leader. How do we control him?"

"While he is a moderate, he is also ambitious," Liz said, having clearly anticipated this question. "If we involve him in the plan to assassinate the current leaders and have evidence of that, we have him."

Alan turned to Paul Weber, one of Donna's field operatives. "Do you have a plan yet to remove the incumbents?"

"Our timescale is three months away. In February, the Supreme Leader and president are planning a visit and official opening of the northern drone manufacturing facility."

Alan was surprised. "That's been open for a year or two."

Paul grinned. "Yes. But they want a photo op. Our asset at the plant, Iran #46, fed us the date of the planned ceremony. He knows nothing about what we're planning, but when I asked if he could fashion an accident that would kill both the Ayatollah and the president, he was ecstatic."

Alan looked up from his laptop. "Details?"

Paul filled him in.

They discussed the plan and various options, then identified areas of risk and things that could go wrong.

"It's not perfect," Alan said, "but I think you've come up with the best possible solution. Congratulations and well done. Now I want a backup plan. If something goes south, what do we do instead?"

Paul laid out a Plan B.

Alan nodded and looked at his watch. "I have the China team in fifteen minutes. Anything else?"

———⚬∞⚬———

While waiting for the next team, Alan looked across at Silvia.

"Iran looks good. We might just pull this off."

She looked up. "I wish we knew more about the Global Strike timetable. If they launch their attack before we implement our plans, all of this will have been for nothing. And I'd also like to know more details of their battle plans."

Chapter Twelve

President Yang sat in his war room in the presidential palace in Beijing. With him were two generals and three simultaneous translators, and he was waiting to commence a video call with the three other members of the Gang of Four.

Yang preferred interacting with one country's leadership at a time, and normally, this was possible. Although there was still a level of suspicion and argument in these sessions, they always ended up with an agreement on the path ahead.

Meeting all three in a joint session was more taxing, and the Chinese president hated these sessions. Over the past few months, he had held only three such meetings, and each had been scheduled for one hour. However, with the translation, fighting, name-calling, and vacillation, the time had usually extended to two or more.

The Chinese president's goal in this meeting would be to lay out a timetable for the strike.

Yang's thoughts were interrupted by a senior aide, who announced that the other leaders had joined the conference. Yang put on a broad smile which, he was sure, displayed sincerity. He aimed it at the camera.

"Gentlemen, welcome to our meeting."

The other leaders grunted.

"I am excited that we are close to launching our attack. My generals and I have worked closely with each of you separately to scope out your strategies, and we are now ready to set dates for the initial attacks."

He consulted a report in front of him, but this was for show, since he knew the details of the document intimately.

"I have agreed with President Chekov that Russia will launch four hypersonic, tactical nuclear missiles on Kyiv on the evening of February twentieth. On February twenty-second, Iran will fire a long-range nuclear weapon on Tel Aviv. It will penetrate the Iron Dome and destroy most of the city, the Israeli armed forces, and all of Israel's government."

He paused, took a sip of tea, and glanced at the faces of the others on the large screens before him. They were hanging on his every word, almost salivating.

"The West will initially focus on Russia and then on Iran," he continued. "But they will drag their heels as they decide how to deal with each of these two actions. They'll conduct talks with the EU and NATO and with anyone left in Tel Aviv. It will take days, perhaps weeks, for them and their allies to respond. We don't expect other Arab nations to take a stand. They will wimp out, as they always do, and sit on the sidelines. The West will be forced to face a war on two fronts.

"One week after the Russian strike, on February twenty-seventh, you, President Kim, will threaten to unleash missiles on South Korea, but will instead launch ICBMs on the United States. They'll be shot down, of course, but the Americans will go crazy. Their politicians will respond with knee-jerk reactions and the Pentagon will fight within itself for how to contain the situation."

Kim interjected," And when will China pull the trigger, President Yang?"

"China will launch the Taiwan attack directly following the other offensives, on March 1."

"Israel's Iron Dome has defended their country since 2011," the Iranian president interjected. "How do we know if the missile the Russians have supplied us will penetrate it?"

Chekov laughed. "Mr. President, the Iron Dome is old. It comprises ten batteries with four launchers each. Each launcher carries twenty interceptor missiles. Overall, eight hundred interceptors. Sounds formidable, but each interceptor has a speed of only seventeen hundred miles per hour, whereas the Russian hypersonic missile that you'll launch travels at nearly seven thousand miles per hour. Just eighteen minutes after launch, it will explode above Tel Aviv."

Yang was not sure of the math involved, nor the likelihood of success, but it really did not matter. It would distract American attention. If Israel shot it down and retaliated, peace in the Middle East would still be disrupted and the United States would still face a second front after Ukraine. Kim's ICBM launch would add the next distraction.

Yang again smiled at his co-conspirators. "That's the first phase for each of us. Now, let's discuss the follow-up. Your invasion of Poland, Dimitri, your invasion of Iraq, President Moradi, your absorption of South Korea, President Kim, and, my occupation of the entire South China Sea and Japan."

Chekov grinned. Yang knew that success in battle had long eluded the Russian, but this plan offered promise of a path ahead.

They were not aware that some forty-eight hundred miles from Moscow, at that very minute, a team of froggies was presenting a plan to eliminate him and destroy the Gang of Four.

Chapter Thirteen

Vivienne La Croix was French, and had previously worked for the DGSE in Paris. She was fluent in Russian, and in her role at the French intelligence agency, she had specialized in developing dossiers on the Russian president and other key members of his cabinet. At Purple Frog, she continued this work and now understood the current Russian president better than anyone.

She was well aware of Chekov's paranoia—or perhaps it was a realistic fear for his life. The Russian had surrounded himself with resources that safeguarded his safety, riding in an armor-plated train, sitting well away from people he was talking with, wearing gloves when shaking hands with others, and always being surrounded by at least four bodyguards, who had been trained by the Spetsnaz before taking their role with Chekov. Vivienne worked closely with Donna Strickland to develop a plot that would eliminate the Russian.

Since the president no longer appeared in public, a long-range rifle shot was out. They considered dozens of scenarios, but each was found to be infeasible.

"The damned man is untouchable," Donna said, frustrated. "And Alan prefers a death that can be classed as an accident or from natural causes. That makes it even harder."

Vivienne cursed." Merde. But speaking of natural causes, he does have a heart problem. He had a bad attack a year ago, which was not widely reported. If he died from that, it would certainly count as a natural cause."

Donna snorted. "Maybe we can scare him to death."

David Osler, fondly known by the froggies as Q, was attending the meeting and looked up. "Something comes to mind. Please excuse me for a half hour and I may be able to solve your problem."

Vivienne motioned to the others in the task force. "Let's take a break. We'll reconvene in forty minutes. Does that work for you, Q?"

"That'll be fine."

When they met again, Q took the floor. "I've confirmed what I remembered. I researched the dark web and found a formula for an aconite derivative that will induce a heart attack in people who are susceptible. It sounds like it would work with Dimitri Chekov. Oh, and it is very hard to detect."

Vivienne looked puzzled. "You Googled it? You keyed in 'Undetectable murder poison?' "

Q rolled his eyes. "Not the conventional web; the dark web. The entries are not indexed and don't show using a traditional browser. But use Tor and all is revealed. Mainly drug trafficking, cyber currency, ransomware, scams, assassins. Anything illegal, and a smattering of legal sites as well. This derivative should do what we want."

Donna showed her skepticism. "If we use this…poison…won't an autopsy reveal it?"

Q shook his head. "No. It shows almost no signs of its presence. Aconite is plant-based and is often called wolfsbane or monkshood. It works on the heart and the nervous system. It would take a very thorough autopsy to detect it, and only if the medic performing it suspected its presence. Most medics will class it as death by heart attack and not check the toxicity. Chekov's death will throw the Kremlin into turmoil as everyone jockeys for power. Calling it 'natural causes' will likely be expedient with a simple autopsy."

Vivienne shook her head. "One problem will be finding a way to administer the drug. He keeps his blood pressure medication in a safe and has someone who tastes all his food and drink. He wears gloves most of the time, so we can't even use a contact version of the drug."

Alan had been observing the conversation and now asked, "Can we coat a glass or his cutlery with it?"

Q keyed a few words into his laptop. "No. We need to administer about an ounce of the drug for it to be effective. Coating on a glass will never be enough."

Alan then asked what all of them had been thinking. "If we include it in something Chekov will eat or drink, the food taster will also get it. Will death be immediate?"

Q looked up from his laptop. "No. It'll take about fifteen minutes."

"Will this kill the food taster as well?"

Q angled his head to one side. "Not necessarily. Chekov has a cardiovascular problem which makes him more susceptible. The food taster is probably younger, and the effects might be minimal or none."

Alan became serious. "So, we administer it in a drink. The taster samples the drink and shows no symptoms. Chekov drinks and a quarter of an hour later, he dies, and perhaps the taster does as well."

Silvia, who had joined the meeting, was outraged. "Good God. We can't do that. It's a heartless murder of the taster. There must be another way."

"Silvia, as Jason said way back, Chekov is effectively murdering several hundred of his citizens in his stupid war every day," Alan countered. "This sacrifice of one man or woman may prevent that."

"We know that Chekov drinks a lot, right?" Q interrupted. Vivienne nodded her agreement. "If we add the drug to a bottle of vodka, the taster will sample it and drink perhaps a single shot. But Chekov will consume a lot more. The dosage for the taster will be minimal."

La Croix consulted her notes. "Chekov drinks a lot. He has a new bottle opened every night and consumes most of it before, during, and after dinner. Anything left over is disposed of. A new, sealed bottle every night."

"How do we get a doctored bottle to him?" Q shook his head.

Alan smiled. "Our new best friend, Boris Menklov, will meet him and offer him a gift."

"And that'll also implicate him in the plot."

Alan nodded. "Let's move to Mr. Menklov."

He paused a moment, then continued.

"Menklov was the first man we identified as a possible replacement for Chekov. Did you consider others, Vivienne?"

"Oui, Alan. The deputy prime minister, several of the generals, the head of the FSB, and the leader of the opposition party, Anton Laski, who, as you know, is in prison."

"So, why Menklov?"

"Process of elimination. We need someone strong enough to move rapidly and ruthlessly deal with Chekov's allies. The Deputy PM is fiercely loyal to Chekov. The generals all want to keep the war going. That's what generals do."

"The head of the FSB?"

"He's a puppeteer. He wants to have power, but he wants it behind the scenes. He has no interest in the position of leadership."

Ching, who had been silent until now, asked, "Laski?"

"Even if we spring him from prison," Vivienne answered, "he'd have a hard time coping with Chekov's thugs. If we had Menklov do all the nasty stuff after Chekov's death, then turn over power to Laski, it would work. But Menklov is not going to agree to that."

Alan made a few notes, then said, "Okay. Tell me what you have on Menklov."

Vivienne consulted her notes. "He is an oligarch worth about four billion dollars. Two billion of his wealth is in offshore accounts, and the sanctions have been unable to locate and freeze these. He lives in Moscow and has a dacha in Barvikha."

"So," Alan asked, "how do we compromise him?"

"He's known for being against the war in Ukraine, and Chekov has added him to his list of probable traitors. Menklov knows this and has kept a very low profile. If we can get him into power, he'll very likely pull out of Ukraine if we encourage him to do so."

"How do we encourage him?"

Vivienne slapped her hand down on the table. "Money. The West can't freeze all of his assets, but we might be able to."

A member of Vivienne's team, Judy Leonardis, was from Tyler Waylon's Money Laundering group. She was an attractive, red-haired, freckled woman with blue eyes and a long history of tracking money laundering operations for the U.S. Treasury.

She smiled at Vivienne. "Actually, I've been working on that already."

She turned to address the team.

"It wasn't easy. I've located his offshore accounts, and he has set up a very complex web of these. If he had one or two accounts, it would be simple, but he holds his money in about a hundred different banks spread all over the world. Malta, Cypress, the BVI, the Caymans, Panama, you name a country with loose fiscal controls and a reputation for hiding money, and he uses it."

"Can we even get to him?" Alan asked. "With that many accounts, it'll take Ching and his team months."

"Agreed. And if we wanted to divert all his money somewhere else, that would take a lot of time and be a major headache."

She looked up from her notes.

"But we don't want to access all his funds; we just want to scare him. Convince him we could do that. If we attack just three of his banks and remove his funds, the threat of doing the same elsewhere should bring him to heel."

Vivienne peered at Judy through her heavy tortoiseshell eyeglasses. "Bring him to heel?"

"It's a dog term. Don't you have dogs?"

"Certainly not."

Judy laughed. "I used to train them before I went to the Treasury."

"Okay," Alan interrupted, "we choose three banks from different geographies to make the point. They shouldn't be ones he believes are the easiest. Put together a list and you can get started."

Leonardis looked at Ching Tong. "I'll need one of your hackers, Ching."

Ching Tong nodded and said, "Jim Barlow would be perfect. I'll tell him to meet you."

"Okay, let's get moving," Alan said. "I have the China team up next."

"On it, Alan."

Chapter Fourteen

While the plans for three of the countries were developing well and starting to look feasible, China's was not.

The China team leader, Ken Lin, looked around and caught Donna's eye. He motioned for her to address the group. "The problem," she said, "is eliminating Yang."

Donna paused for a moment, then continued.

"The intel that we have indicates that he hardly ever leaves the presidential palace these days. He sleeps there, has his office there, and seems to be adopting a bunker mentality probably until Global Strike starts."

"So, we have to get to him in the palace."

"We have no intel on that, and the CIA hasn't been able to help."

Alan stood and started pacing the conference room. He shook his head. Even if the other countries' strategies worked, if Yang survived, a major player would still be in place. Global Strike might be called off, but China would remain a major threat and would probably attempt to renew the Gang of Four pact.

"So, we have to eliminate him in the palace, and no one knows how his security works there. Right?"

"Right."

Then a thought struck him. Alan knew a man who had met with Yang in the palace and might have a view on the security and its vulnerability.

"November Swan," he said, and Donna and the other members of the team looked at him inquisitively.

"Swan met with Yang when he was doing the rare earth negotiations. He may not have noticed anything about Yang's security measures, but then, he may have. Knowing the man, I'll bet he noticed everything."

Donna nodded. "So, how do we find him?"

"According to Tina, he was in Thailand a few months ago. In Phuket." Alan reached for the intercom and spoke Ching Tong's name.

Ching came on the line.

"Ching, can you locate November Swan for me? He was in Phuket a few months ago."

"I'll try."

"Don't try, do it."

"Yes, boss."

The team disbursed, and an hour later, Ching called Alan back. "Tracked some brokerage transactions, found his smartphone number, and triangulated the cell towers. He's still in Phuket and I have an address."

Donna was with Alan and smiled. "I'll pack three swimsuits."

November Swan, once the third richest person in the world, had been forced to swap his life of wealth for one where his expenditure was just a few dollars a day. Novi, as he was known, now lived in a small ramshackle house on the beach at Ya Nui on the island of Phuket in Thailand. The house had a single large room in which a couple of old couches shared the space with a kitchen, table, chairs, and a bed. The shower was outside, as was the toilet, behind a bamboo screen.

The American woke late and walked out onto the white sand. The Andaman Sea lapped gently at the shoreline, and he thought of the breakfast that Angie was out buying. He was barefoot and walked into the water, feeling its cooling effect.

Turning, he walked leisurely back to the house and settled in front of his laptop, checking the world news. He was delighted that his cellphone-based internet connection was working. Although slow, it had an acceptable speed.

"Hi, darlin'." Angie had returned with their breakfast, which was still warm from when the street food man had prepared it.

He returned her greeting. "Hi, darlin'."

She was beautiful. A few years younger than him—actually, twenty-nine. She was a New Zealander with a master's degree in engineering. Dressed in a small, white bikini, she had added a coverup for her ten-minute walk into town.

"Aroon was cooking Indonesian food today—a shrimp goreng. Odd breakfast, but it looks and smells good."

"Do you think you're safe walking around like that? You have such a hot body, and your bikini doesn't hide much. Some guy is going to jump you."

"Let him try." Her muscles were toned from daily weight training, and she had serious martial arts credentials. Novi laughed.

She looked about her. "This is paradise. I could spend the rest of my life here."

Novi looked about. He agreed, feeling happier than at any other time in his life.

"Get it while it's hot," she said.

After breakfast, they took a swim for a half hour, then Novi returned to his laptop.

She stood beside him in their main room. "What do you do all day, Novi? You spend hours on that computer of yours." She laughed. "I know. You're playing the stock market. You're trading your two billion dollars and cranking it up to, what, four billion?"

"Actually, five."

"You're living in cloud cuckoo land. No one has two billion dollars, and certainly not five billion."

"Actually, I'm not, and I do."

He closed his laptop and reached over to her, releasing the top of her bikini. As he ran his hands over her breasts, she moaned. "And what do you want?" she asked him.

"You should know by now."

What neither of them knew was that two Chinese nationals had landed at Phuket airport early that morning and would soon be on their way to the village where Novi and his partner were living.

The Chinese were officers in the State Security Ministry, but used passports that described them as academics. Since each was heavily muscled and had scars from previous fights, their cover identity was dubious. The immigration officials at Phuket Airport were suspicious, but their documents appeared to be in order, and they had been instructed to welcome visitors who brought currency and supported the local businesses.

"Welcome to Phuket, gentlemen."

The pair hailed a taxi and told the driver they would be staying at the Ritsurin Boughtique in Phuket Town. The driver attempted to have them change to another hotel where he received a commission.

"You want hotel on beach? Ritsurin in town. Not on beach. I have better hotel."

The two men sitting in the back of the old Mercedes taxi wore sunglasses, and though they wore light clothes, they did not appear to be tourists. The driver had always delighted in assessing the characters of his passengers, and he correctly viewed these men as dangerous. The one who seemed in charge was taller and better looking. The other was shorter, had several scars on the left side of his face, and gave the impression of being a cruel individual. They ignored his sales pitch, so the driver shrugged and started his vehicle.

Each of the Chinese officers took a private room in the modern, well-appointed hotel. They met in the taller man's room to discuss their next steps, but before doing so, they used instruments they had brought with them to check for listening devices. As they expected, they found none.

The shorter agent asked, "Who is this Swan man?"

"That's not in the briefing. Our orders are simple, though. Find him and kill him. And kill him painfully. The order came directly from the Presidential Palace."

"President Yang must be really pissed with this man."

The tall man nodded. "The rumor is that, last year, he caused great embarrassment between the president and Russia."

"Who cares about Russia? They are a failed nation."

The taller agent was starting to become annoyed by his companion. "President Yang has lost face and that is a big deal. Anyway, we have our orders, and we'll carry them out. Okay?"

"Okay. So where do we find this American?"

"He rents a house on Ya Nui. We'll go there tomorrow and kill him."

The shorter agent smiled. "But tonight, let's have some fun. This is a party town, I'm told. I want a woman to make me happy."

The agent in charge spat on the floor. "You are disgusting, Duan. All you think about is your cock."

"Don't forget my other specialty: I inflict pain. This man will spend many hours regretting whatever he did to President Yang."

The taller agent grunted. "I despise your skills, but I could never do what you do. That's why they sent you with me. But I am not going out whoring with you tonight. And you aren't going alone, either. This is a mission. Maybe when we are done, you can have a treat. A bonus."

"Okay. When I have killed him, I'll be really in the mood for—"

"Breakfast tomorrow," the senior agent interrupted. His real name was Li, although his passport did not identify him as such. "Seven a.m."

The following day, they ate an American-style breakfast of eggs and bacon as Li used a map app on his cellphone to locate Novi's house.

"We'll rent a car," he told Duan. "I have already asked the man at reception to organize it."

Chapter Fifteen

An hour later, the two Chinese agents drove to Ya Nui beach and identified the house they had been told was rented by November Swan. They saw a tall, beautiful blonde woman come out of the house, followed by a man they recognized from a photograph in their briefing file. It was their target. Swan and the woman stepped into an old Jeep and drove off towards Phuket Town.

Li had been curious about this man, and the night before, he had looked him up on the internet, which he could not do when they were in mainland China. It surprised him that their target had once been the third richest person on the planet. A man now sought by the U.S. authorities. A criminal.

The Chinese agent felt certain that the man still had access to significant wealth, and decided that when the American was suffering at his hands, he would discover where he had hidden his money. The file indicated that his bosses in Beijing suspected his wealth, but knew no way of accessing it. If Li could find the secret, he might become a rich man. He thought about sharing with Duan. *Perhaps.*

Li and Duan scouted the location and came up with a plan. It was simple. The house was in a remote and unpopulated area, the American did not have any bodyguards, and the woman would not be a threat. They decided to enter the house when the man was home and confront him.

Duan smiled. "We'll wait for them. I want the woman to be at home as well as Swan. I'll have fun with her."

In the early afternoon, Novi and Angie returned from shopping and unloaded their groceries.

The two Chinese agents watched as the couple carried two straw baskets of food into the small house.

Li signaled to Duan. "Let's go."

They walked quickly to the house and unholstered their QSZ-92 handguns. From what Li had read, all Americans carried handguns, rifles, and even assault weapons, so Li decided not to take a chance.

As the Chinese man entered the main room of the house, Novi saw the drawn handguns and his jaw dropped open. He raised his hands. "What do you want? Are you the police?"

Li spoke reasonable English, but Duan, the shorter agent, did not speak the language at all. Duan looked at his superior with curiosity about what was being said.

"We not police. We…" Li hesitated, attempting to remember the English equivalents of what he wanted to say. "…come from China. President Yang not happy with you."

Novi was angry now. "I lost everything, and I committed treason against the U.S. because of him. Yang may not be happy with me, but I'm not happy with *him*."

Angie, who had also raised her hands, looked surprised. "Novi, what's happening?"

"It's okay, darling. I'm sure it's a misunderstanding," he lied.

Duan spoke to his colleague in Mandarin. "What's he saying?"

Li found Duan's interference annoying and told him to shut up.

He looked around for a computer, which he assumed the American used to access his funds.

"Where your computer?"

Novi had locked it in a safe while they were out and wondered what the Chinese man wanted with it. He knew that the longer he could delay them, the more likely it was that someone else would happen along, although the house was on a deserted stretch of the coastline and they had few visitors.

"Why do you want my laptop?"

Li let out a laugh. "Not you to know. Get it."

Duan asked again and Li lost his patience with the man.

"Leave this to me. Keep them covered, but I'll talk with him and get what I need."

Duan grunted his reluctant acceptance of his taller colleague's order.

Angie lowered her hands. "I'm getting fed up with these creeps, Novi. Tell them to bugger off."

Novi glared at her. "It's not that easy."

"Oh, yes, it is." She stepped forward and delivered a sharp jab to Duan's throat, then kicked her foot out, delivering a strong blow to his groin. Duan exhaled and sank to the floor, his handgun spilling from his grasp.

Li turned his gun and aimed it at her, but as he was about to pull the trigger, Novi threw himself at the man, deflecting his aim.

Novi had only been in a physical conflict with another on one occasion, and was unable to counter Li's next move, which was to slam the weapon into Novi's head.

Angie moved to confront the remaining Chinese man, who was waving his gun at her. He motioned for her to step back. She did so.

Novi was dazed and had fallen. Trying to clear his head, he stood to confront the man.

Duan groaned and tried to stand, but failed. He was in pain from his injuries, but was also incensed that they had been inflicted by a young woman, who seemed to be skilled in martial arts.

Li smiled, finding Duan's embarrassment amusing. *Serves you right, you fool.*

He turned to Novi. "My colleague is evil man. Wants your woman. Sex and torture. If you provide access to your money, we not do that."

Angie turned white.

Novi threw out his hands, indicating defeat, and moved to the safe. He opened it, took out his computer, and turned it on. He entered his password, but then shook his head. "The internet is down."

"You lie. Show me?"

In China, Li used a Chinese keyboard and his screen displayed Chinese characters. The Microsoft interface in English that he saw on Novi's system meant nothing to him. Li debated what to do. Was the internet really down, or was the American trying to fool him?

"Duan, tie up the woman." The short man grinned and hit Angie across the head with his weapon, which he had picked up from where he had dropped it. She collapsed and Novi started towards them.

"Stop! No interfere or she die, and you too."

Duan withdrew two zip ties he had brought and secured Angie's hands and ankles. When he had secured her, he stared at her and leered. He started to run his hands over her body.

Novi leaped forward, but Li stopped him.

"You access money, now."

"I told you; the internet is down. I cannot connect to my bank."

Duan ignored the discussion and, feasting his eyes on Angie, continued to run his hands over her. He tore off her bikini top.

Then he heard a female voice with an American accent from behind him "That's not very nice." He grabbed his gun, which he had put down, and turned to face whoever it was behind him. In the back of his mind, he registered a muffled shot. Then the back of his head exploded as brain and bones flew out over Angie's near-naked body.

Li gasped and turned to see an attractive blonde woman standing in the doorway holding a handgun. He raised his own gun in reaction, but the intruder calmly shot him twice in the head.

"Sorry about the mess, Angie. It is Angie, isn't it? I'm Donna." The woman looked down at the two dead Chinese agents.

She freed Angie, who spent the next ten minutes showering, washing the blood and bone fragments from her body, and trying to calm herself. She changed into a long gown that covered her completely, but was still shaking. Novi poured her a brandy and had one himself.

Novi nodded his appreciation for Donna's timely entrance. "Thanks so much. Who are you?"

"I'm Donna Strickland. I work for someone you might remember. Alan Harlan."

"I don't get it. They arrive from nowhere and threaten us with torture and death, and then you show up. And you just killed them. Alan Harlan was a contractor. How would he have a killer working for him?"

"Just thank your lucky stars that I happened to get here when I did. Now, do you have some old towels? There is quite a mess to be cleaned up."

Donna helped Novi clean the room, then he turned to her. "What do we do with them?"

She looked grim. "Do you have a boat?"

They spent nearly three hours disposing of the bodies in the waters off a nearby island, hoping that the fish would remove traces of the men's presence.

However, Donna expected that the bodies would be washed ashore a few miles away and provide a challenge for the local police.

Angie had recovered, but was still shaken. The physical work Novi had undertaken with Donna in disposing of the Chinese agents 'bodies had enabled him to recover more quickly, and now the three of them sat inside. While Novi drank some of the brandy, Angie finished the remains of the bottle. Donna drank some cold water and now addressed the two.

"How are you now? It really was lucky that I arrived when I did. The shorter Chinese man had a whole set of tools on his belt, which I'm guessing he would have used to inflict a lot of suffering."

She poured herself more water from a large plastic bottle and drank it.

"What were they after?"

Novi looked at her. "Revenge on behalf of President Yang in China, and they knew about my wealth. I think they wanted that for themselves."

Angie's eyes widened. "Then you *do* have money?"

"Didn't you look me up?"

"I looked up November Swan, but the pictures of him were completely not you. He didn't have a beard and was always serious. They said he never smiled."

Donna interrupted. "It's better you discuss this after I've gone. I came here for a reason."

"You want money?"

"No. I want information. We are working to remove Yang from office." Donna liked that phrase. Better than "assassinating" him.

"We have no intel on the security he has in the Presidential Palace in Beijing," she continued. "I believe you have been there to meet him."

"Yes. That's right. Several times."

"It'll be very helpful if you can tell me whatever you remember about it."

Novi smiled. "I remember everything. One of my companies was in personal security, so I became an expert. The palace's security was elaborate and sophisticated. All state of the art. Impregnable."

That evening, Donna boarded a flight from Phuket to Washington D.C., connecting through Doha.

Before leaving, she called Alan.

He started the conversation. "How's he doing? He's a villain, but he's very smart."

"Actually, he seems a changed man. Novi's very much in love with a New Zealander, who is really cute. They make a great couple."

"And what about Yang and his security at the palace?"

"Swan gave me the scoop. Yang's palace is built like a vault. I don't see how we can pull off a hit there, so we're going to need another approach."

Chapter Sixteen

Our hundred miles south of Phuket, in Malaysia, a cell phone rang.

Bradley Johnson verified the origin of the call and implemented an encryption sequence. He answered and asked, "What do you want?" He knew the caller and suspected the reason for the call.

The woman in his bed stirred but did not wake.

The voice at the other end of the line did not spend time with personal chitchat, but appeared ready to talk business.

Brad was annoyed. "Hey. It's the middle of the night here, and the bottom line is I'm retired. I can guess what you want, but the answer is 'no'. I haven't been in the business for three years."

The voice on the line spat out a number.

"That's a lot of money, but as I just said, I'm retired." Brad paused. "That size of fee implies a very powerful target. Let me guess. A cartel boss?"

The voice confirmed that the target was indeed a cartel boss and the reason for the requested contract was an affair between him and the client's mistress.

They spoke for a few minutes more and Brad continued to insist that he had no interest, at whatever price, to return to his old life. He was now Bradley Johnson, an Australian, not Abdul, the assassin.

He woke the next morning in their large, antique brass bed and looked around. He always rose early, performed stretching exercises, and then rang for a servant to make and bring coffee. His wife, Betty Lau, always slept until the coffee arrived and the fragrant smell of the black brew awakened her.

"I'm going for a run, darling," he said.

"I don't know why you tell me that every day. You always go for run." She smiled at him. "Sex when you get back?"

"We always do that as well." He returned her smile.

Their estate was in the hills above Penang in Malaysia. They had bought the property three years before, when it was little more than a ruin with most of the existing masonry covered by vines and other jungle foliage. Over the first two years, he and his wife had supervised the reconstruction and extension of the property so that now the palatial house retained its traditional features but boasted new plumbing and electricity. It was freshly painted, airy, and the grounds were well-kept.

Chain wire fencing ringed the twenty-acre estate, and fifty security cameras were hidden, covering the perimeter. Brad had erected signs shouting out "do not enter" messages in Malay as a deterrent to burglars. He'd designed the security aspects of their home to provide adequate protection from any individuals who might attempt to harm them.

Normal people required protection, but it was often tertiary. Betty, as well as having a string of fashion boutiques throughout the East, was the leader of a Chinese gang based in Shanghai, and her husband, whom she still called Brad, had been known as an acclaimed assassin. On the world stage, the name 'Abdul' solicited fear or admiration, depending on whether you were a recipient or a buyer of the man's services.

Two men always accompanied him on his morning run within the perimeter of his home, but on narrow paths through the jungle.

He had completed the first mile when he heard gunfire. It came from the house, and his two bodyguards drew Sig Sauer automatics, passed a third to their boss, and took up positions to defend him, if necessary.

Brad called to them," It's coming from the house. Let's get back there. I don't want Betty hurt."

They ran back to the house where silence had again descended, the only sound being the usual calls of birds crying out their songs.

The front door was open, and his two bodyguards took covering positions as they entered. They immediately saw the bodies of three other bodyguards, who had stayed with Betty. They lay dead on the floor of the broad entrance hall.

Brad kept his handgun in an alert position, having chambered a round and removed the safety catch. He strode up to the bedroom past a servant who lay dead on the stairs.

Inside, he found Betty. A series of bullet wounds ran across her thin, naked body, and her eyes were open and filled with surprise.

"Oh, God."

He took his dead wife in his arms and cried.

His bodyguards searched the house and found other bodies. They also found a number of the servants who had hidden and evaded the killers. They told Brad about the incursion.

A call had been received from the main gate by a woman who seemed to be in distress. A servant had gone out to help her and was overpowered as the attackers streamed in through the open gate. A cowardly attack by a group of eight men who appeared to be Chinese had followed.

One of the bodyguards retrieved video from the security system and this corroborated the servants' story.

Abdul laid Betty's lifeless body back on the bed where she had met her end and called to his head bodyguard. "Who did this?"

"We don't know, sir. They were professionals. They made a clean escape afterwards, but one of my men must have gotten lucky and killed one of them. I checked and he carried a smartphone with him."

"Why would he come into action with something like that?"

"I don't know. Sloppy? Or maybe they used smartphones for communicating."

Brad felt himself transitioning from the quiet, dedicated husband he had become in the past three years. Now, Bradley Johnson was gone and the man who stood talking with his bodyguards was the coldstone killer, Abdul.

The bodyguard continued. "I tried to open the phone, but it's locked. I don't have the skills to break into it."

Abdul said, "I don't have the skills, either." Then a memory flashed through his mind and he added, "But I know someone who does."

Silvia was surprised when one of the many smartphones she kept for operations rang. It had a telephone number that had been dormant for several years, and had last been used when Purple Frog had contracted an external assassin to help with a mission related to Venezuela.

She triggered the voice modification software and answered the phone.

"Who is this?" she asked.

"My name is Abdul. You may remember me. Did you send your hitmen to kill my wife?"

She gasped and said," God. That was not us. I'm so sorry. What happened?"

They spoke for about ten minutes and Abdul accepted that the death of his wife had not been sanctioned by the person he was speaking with.

Silvia asked him. "Is there a way we can help?"

He paused, then replied, "Yes. I need a phone hacked."

Later that day, Abdul couriered the killer's smartphone to a mailbox in Reston, Virginia. A day later, he received a call from a hacker who had cracked the phone and wanted to know what information he needed.

"Hello," the hacker said. "We met briefly in California a few years ago."

The voice had an American accent, but Abdul remembered the Chinese hacker he had met on that trip.

"Ching?"

"Yes."

"Any luck with the phone?"

"Of course. Child's play."

"And?"

"What do you want to know?"

"What was his name and what else was on his phone?"

"Lots of low-level stuff. I don't think your dead man was the leader of the hit team, and I don't think he was supposed to carry the phone with him. His name was Jian. He was Chinese."

He heard Ching consulting some notes.

"Most of his calls were in Shanghai," Ching continued, "so I did some surfing and accessed a few databases, including one in the Shanghai police department. Jian was a member of a gang, The Blue Angel. He communicated a lot with the head man, Guo Liu. Mean anything?"

"Yes. My wife was linked to a gang in Shanghai and the Blue Angel was their main rival. She bettered Guo in a number of deals. That bastard was out for revenge."

Abdul was now seething with rage and spat into the phone," Can you find where Guo Liu is?"

"No problem. I have his number from Jian's contacts. I'll triangulate from the cell towers to find him. I'll call you back when I have something."

A half-hour later, Ching Tong called Abdul again. "He's currently in Shanghai, and I have an address."

A week later, Abdul, traveling as Bradley Johnson, arrived at Shanghai's Pudong International Airport. He was met by members of Betty's gang, whom he knew from previous excursions to China.

The head of the gang, who spoke good English, briefed him on what he knew. "Guo Liu is boss of Blue Angel gang. He has fortune from various illegal activities and has paid off the local police sufficiently to be able to operate in the open. He wears most expensive designer clothes and shoes and dines out at top Shanghai restaurants."

Abdul listened and took notes as the man continued.

"He well known in Chinese society as being villain and most people avoid contact with him whenever they can. Restaurant owners did not like having him as customer and one banned him from the establishment. That owner was found a day later disemboweled in the restaurant kitchen. The message was clear, and the restaurant owners now do not refuse him."

"What's his schedule like?" Abdul asked. "When he goes out, is he armed? Bodyguards?"

"Guo always travels in small convoy of vehicles with ten bodyguards. He know many people hate him, and most would like revenge for the wrongs he has done to them, so he takes his security seriously."

The head of Betty's gang continued the briefing with more details, answering Abdul's questions about Guo's habits. He pledged to assist Abdul in every way possible to avenge his previous boss's death.

"Ms. Lau was mother to me and to all in gang. We avenge her death even if we all die doing."

Abdul contemplated a long-range rifle shot, which was his specialty, but the burning rage he felt for the man made him decide to find a plan that would be up close and personal.

He decided to check out what he had been told and traveled to the Huangpu area of Shanghai. Using high-power binoculars, he checked out the motorcade which Guo Liu used when he left his apartment. It comprised three vehicles, with five bodyguards in the lead vehicle, an SUV, and another five in an SUV at the rear. Guo Liu rode alone or with one of several women he frequented in the center in an expensive American limousine. He was accompanied only by the driver.

Abdul discovered that the limousine was leased from a dealer in the Shanghai suburbs, and if there were any issues, such as a minor accident or a dirty vehicle, the leasing company provided a replacement within an hour.

One week after Abdul's arrival in the Chinese city, Guo's limo was found to have been vandalized, with serious scrapes and graffiti across the doors and hood. The driver called the limousine company and a replacement was delivered twenty minutes later.

That evening, Guo Liu left his apartment and his driver opened the rear door for him.

On entering, the gang boss immediately raised the opaque privacy divider and settled back for the fifteen-minute drive to the Jin Xuan restaurant.

It was nighttime, and the back of the vehicle with its smoked glass windows was dark. Guo settled back in his seat and thought about his empire. He had a few weak players and decided that he would have them removed in the next few days. Removal in Guo's empire was permanent.

He noticed a movement in the empty seats, behind the driver and facing him, and swore in Mandarin, "What the fuck?"

The seat separated and a man, dressed in black and with a blackened face, reached out and slashed the gang boss across the throat with a razor-sharp knife. Guo recognized the blade as a Japanese short sword, a Wakizashi. His English was poor, but he understood the words that the darkened man uttered. "This is from Betty."

Abdul picked up the communications microphone and spoke to the driver, who had realized that something was amiss. "I understand you speak English."

"Yes. But who are you? Where is Guo Liu?"

"Guo Liu has departed this world, and if you do not want to accompany him, listen closely to my orders. I do not wish to harm you."

The man in the front seat was terrified. "I just drive. Tell me what you want me to do and I'll do it."

Abdul looked out at the streets they were passing and consulted a map app.

"Turn right at the second cross street."

The driver did so and the SUV in their rear followed them. The lead vehicle had continued straight and the bodyguards likely realized they'd lost their boss's limousine. Abdul saw the vehicle stop and start to turn around .

He looked out the back window and saw that the SUV behind him was gaining. A smartphone that Guo carried started to ring. Abdul ignored it and motioned to the driver." Pull up level with that white building and stop."

The driver did so and Abdul sprang out of the vehicle and ran up the steps into the deserted facility. The trailing SUV also stopped and the bodyguards emerged and ran to the limo. They looked inside and saw Guo Liu's lifeless body.

The senior bodyguard screamed in Mandarin, "He went in there. Let's go!"

They entered the building, but as they ran forward with guns drawn, a barrage of fire cut them down as Betty's gang members took their revenge.

The lead SUV had now drawn up outside and the five bodyguards from this vehicle replicated their colleagues 'mistake and were also killed as they entered the facility.

Abdul went outside and talked to the limousine driver.

"Our fight is not with you. Go home. Tell the gang members everything that happened here if they ask."

"Thank you, sir. But I think leaving Shanghai tonight might be a better move for me." He paused, then said. "Is Guo Liu dead?"

Abdul pointed at the bloodied corpse. "What do you think?"

Three days later, the severed head of Guo Liu was delivered to his family, along with threats of what would happen if they attempted any retaliation.

As he was leaving Pudong airport for Kuala Lumpur, Abdul remembered his last discussion before leaving Malaysia. It had been with the head of the mysterious organization which had identified Guo Liu. She had said to him, "We're happy to help you on this one, Abdul, but there will be a quid pro quo. There is a job we may want you to undertake for us."

Chapter Seventeen

Ginny Krangle from Profiling did not live with Ching Tong, but there were few nights when they did not spend the night with each other, either in his apartment or hers. They had been dating for nearly a year.

As they sat on her couch, Ching looked across at his partner. "The plans for three of the countries are just about complete. It's just China that remains a challenge."

Ginny smiled. "I heard that. So how are we going to do it?"

"I don't know, but Alan and Donna spent the afternoon working on it, and when they left for the night, it looked like they had cracked it. Ginny, we're taking over the world."

"Scary stuff. Are you okay with this, Ching?"

"Kind of."

"If we can pull it off, we'll have made an amazing step towards world peace." She placed her hands on his and looked over at him.

He nodded. "Yes, but it will probably be temporary. The bastards we'll put in power will move heaven and earth to find a way of getting out from under our control, and I'm sure even as we use all the tricks in the book, they'll eventually succeed."

She snuggled up to him. "But, in the interim, we'll have done good. There's still a lot we need to do. And let's hope we can pull it off."

He reached for her. "Right now, I have other thoughts." He kissed her on the neck, then on the lips.

It was an odd relationship. He was Chinese and she was Spanish. He was short and a little overweight. She was tall and slender. His face was nondescript whereas hers was angled. She could have been a model. She was forty and he was a mere twenty-seven. In his role as a hacker, he dealt with precision and numeric accuracy. As a profiler, she developed scenarios filled with facts and overlaid with insight that her creativity developed.

But there was something else going on that neither could isolate, and it drew them to one another: they were in love.

She reached over and started to undress him.

Alan met with Silvia the next day and explained his idea for eliminating Yang.

Silvia played with a pen she had been doodling with as Alan spoke. "Not a perfect solution, but it'll get the job done."

She sat back in her chair, then looked at the large screens about the conference room, all filled with details of their plans for each of the four countries.

"My God, Alan. It might all work. I'll bring Jason up to date."

Jason was ecstatic. "That's terrific! I want to go over the details, and we'll need some serious time to work through each of the plans. I'll fly up tomorrow and be in the office by late morning."

The next day, Jason flew into the Washington area. A limousine met him at the Dulles Airport private jet terminal and drove him to a restaurant about two miles from the Purple Frog headquarters, where he transferred to a battered SUV.

The driver held the door open for him. "Good morning, Mr. Overly."

"Morning, Jim."

They drove to the shabby exterior of a single-story building in rural Virginia. It was set in a field of uncut grass and shrubs. It looked deserted and in need of a coat of paint. It appeared to be unoccupied, and there was no obvious security. A single, rusted chain prevented vehicular access to the site.

As the SUV approached, the chain, driven by an electric motor, lowered to the ground to allow access and a shipping-sized door in the building opened. The SUV entered the building and drove down a steep ramp to a massive car park with about seventy vehicles—the transportation for each of the froggies who worked in the building.

The outer door closed quietly. Jason left the vehicle and walked past a small guard office to the steps leading to the main office area of Purple Frog.

He strode with confidence, believing that this day, he would agree on the plans with Silvia and Alan and move ahead with them. While he could have easily taken the meeting by videoconference from St. Croix, he knew this meeting was of such importance that face-to-face contact was essential.

"Good morning, Jason," Silvia greeted him as he entered the main conference room.

"Morning, Silvia, Alan."

Alan put the finishing touches on an espresso and handed it to the billionaire.

Jason took the small cup. "Thanks. Okay, let's start."

Silvia led off. "As we discussed by phone, we have plans for each of the Global Strike countries. It's going to be difficult, and there are a lot of things that could go wrong." She turned to Alan. "Take us through each country plan, please, Alan."

Over the next three hours, Jason was merciless, grilling Alan on the details of each country's plan and the contingency plans for when some things went wrong.

Finally, he said, "Outstanding work. I think you have it cracked. Do you have a timetable for implementation?"

"Each country will take some time to set up. Compromising the replacement leader will take the longest, so we have the assassinations tentatively planned for early next year."

"Will you implement them all together? Same day?"

"No, that would squeeze us too thin. Anything that goes wrong will need attention, so we plan to do them sequentially. But over a week or two in February."

"Do you have a sequence decided?"

"We'll implement the easier ones first: Iran and North Korea. At the very least, disruption in these countries will slow down the overall Global Strike plan."

Jason had finished his coffee and held up his cup for Alan to prepare another. "Are you happy with all this, Silvia?"

"Yes. I still have concerns. If we get this done, we'll end up with enormous power, and we need to be able to manage that. We'll be playing God."

She put her coffee cup down and continued.

"But I can live with that. Alan's always been a pragmatist, and I guess I'm becoming one, too."

Jason laughed. "Good. So, we'll have created a benevolent dictatorship."

Silvia scowled. "As long as it's benevolent."

Jason looked at his two colleagues. "We're going to do this together. We three. And I wouldn't be happy if it was anyone else but you two."

After the meeting with Jason, Alan started the recruitment of the replacement presidents.

His attempt in China ran into difficulty, so he and Silvia held a conference call with Jason. "Yang has purged all his opposition," he said, "so we'll need to recruit someone who currently has significant loyalty to the man. We've profiled several candidates, but none of them seem viable. Contacting any of them will be tricky, and we could blow the whole operation."

"I know someone who might be able to help," Jason said.

Alan laughed, thinking immediately of the Chinese billionaire. "Of course."

Later that day, Jason briefed Henry Ju-long on a few of the elements of Operation Switch.

"So, old friend, who is the best candidate?" he finished. "We need someone who will agree to the elimination of Yang, be prepared to step in and initiate policies to reduce the world-wide threat level significantly. Any ideas?"

Henry let out a laugh. "Pragmatically, the Chinese premier is next in overall power within China after the president. Premier Huang Wei has held his position for several years, and comes from a family with deep links to both members throughout the party and with important individuals in the Chinese business world. But perhaps…" He paused a moment." Leave this to me."

Huang and Henry were close friends, and the Chinese premier was not surprised when Henry suggested they meet at an upmarket restaurant in a fashionable area of Beijing.

Huang always traveled with a bodyguard detail, and the evening when he dined with Henry was no exception.

Henry had arranged a private room. The bodyguards waited outside, and Henry and the premier started the evening with Ardbeg 10 Year Old Scotch whisky, one of Huang's not so secret indulgences.

Huang came quickly to the point." Henry, it's been a long time since we dined out together and I suspect this is not just a social meeting."

Henry leaned forward and whispered, "Global Strike."

Huang looked confused. "Global strike?"

"You don't know about that?"

"About what?"

Henry sighed in relief that his friend was unaware of Yang's plot and not part of it. He spent the next twenty minutes telling Huang the story he had learned from Jack Chen, Huang's face showing more and more alarm as Henry added details to the narrative.

Huang sat back, exhausted. "President Yang disappeared for a few days that week and became evasive when I asked him where he had been. Lately, he's been more remote than ever, and whenever we speak, he seems obsessed with China's military strength. This now makes sense. It also explains the troop movements and secret meetings between Yang and his top generals."

"What's your view on this Global Strike?" Henry asked. "Is it something China should be doing?"

"Certainly not. My country is most important to me, and we must continue our battle with the West. But we should do that with economic measures and cyber-attacks. Not face-to-face fighting and killing. This craziness will end up with millions dying. The world will be set back hundreds of years, if it even survives."

Huang sat forward in his chair.

"Yang's ambition will be the end of China. But I cannot think of how we can persuade him to drop this venture."

Henry leaned closer to his friend and lowered his voice. "If Yang is deposed in some way, would you be prepared to take power and agree to various measures to foster world peace?"

"Are you suggesting a coup?"

Chapter Eighteen

Alan read the email he had received from Henry and smiled. Then he turned back to the file Vivienne had prepared on their candidate for the Russian replacement.

Boris Menklov had served in the KGB with Chekov, and had also been a close ally of the earlier Russian president, Dobry Petrovski. Petrovski had rewarded Menklov's loyalty by selling him a number of state-owned mines for a handful of rubles. The mining operations were actually worth billions of U.S. Dollars, and Petrovski had made it clear that the real owner of the wealth was him, not Menklov. However, Boris could enjoy the proceeds from the operation while he remained loyal to the president.

When Petrovski allegedly committed suicide and Chekov took the presidency, Menklov had switched loyalty to the new leader, and for years, this had satisfied each man. When Chekov launched the Ukrainian invasion, Menklov had seen the folly of the move and believed that the operation would fail. He saw that the war would likely bring down the Russian state, but he did not voice his opinion.

Now, well over a year since the operation had started, Menklov had personally suffered significant monetary losses from the West's sanctions. He was bitter, and this was exasperated when his pride and joy—the *Majestic,* a three-hundred-foot mega yacht—was seized by the Spanish authorities.

The Russian administration and the state press and media outlets had always presented information that varied somewhat from the truth, but now the lies were bolder. Conscription, the weak economy, and draconian laws related to speaking out against the Chekov regime grated on many, but particularly Menklov.

With two billion U.S. Dollars in secret offshore accounts, Menklov prepared to leave mother Russia for good. He would live somewhere where he would be somewhat safe from Chekov's rages.

Menklov had a few aides who were totally loyal to him, and he asked one to reach out to various foreign governments where he might choose to live.

A week later, he received a phone message that a realtor outside Russia wanted to have a private telephone call with him.

Menklov asked his aide from which country the realtor had called.

"He was vague, but I think it is the United States."

The call was brief, and Menklov assumed the "realtor" was actually a member of the CIA. The "realtor" said that he guessed that Menklov had an interest in "buying property" in another location and suggested he take a call with "someone from a different department" to discuss some alternatives. Menklov agreed.

A day later, the oligarch received a text message, which was short and innocuous. It instructed him to take an encrypted call over Telegraph.

A further day passed and Menklov started to worry. If the Americans knew about his plans, the FSB surely would as well.

The call came in and the voice laid out a path forward for the Russian. He would not even need to leave Russia. In fact, he would shortly *own* Russia.

Nearly a dozen calls followed as details of the operation were laid out. Menklov's fear of being revealed as a traitor and concerns for the viability of the plot dissolved over time as his greed, vanity, and ambition took over.

A few weeks later, when Jess arrived home, she found Alan packing a suitcase.

"Off somewhere?"

"Not abroad, if that's what you're thinking."

She was silent, her face asking the question.

He folded a shirt and placed it in his case. "Operation Switch has started."

She grimaced. "And your role?"

"I'm managing it. The replacement presidents have already been set up, so that part's done."

"Wow. That must have been tricky."

"It was, and we had a few false starts. Some things worked and others didn't, but today we concluded the last recruitment."

He paused, focusing on the suitcase for a moment.

"Tomorrow and over the next two weeks," he finally continued, "we'll carry out the assassinations. These will be much riskier than the recruitment, and we'll undoubtedly need to make some changes to the operation as it's rolled out. It's unlikely it'll all go as planned. We may have to improvise."

"God, Alan. We discussed this, but surely you aren't going to carry out one of more of these yourself."

"Of course not." He winced, thinking of the members of Purple Frog and their allies who would be risking their lives in this phase while he sat safely in Virginia. "But I need to be on-hand, monitoring the operations and making changes as needed. Silvia and I have set up a command center at the office. For the next two weeks, we'll be there as the reports come in."

"Oh, darling, can I help?"

"Thanks, but this is something I need to do alone. It'll all be over in two weeks, and we shall have succeeded...or failed."

She hugged him. "I love you so much, Alan Harlan. And I'm so proud of you. I have total faith in you. You will succeed!"

He closed his case and swung it off the bed.

She stepped back. "Go kill those fuckers."

"So, Alan, we'll be here for two weeks?"

Alan joined Silvia in the conference room.

"That's right," he said. "Jason will stay in St. Croix, and we'll update him periodically, but you and I and a bunch of the froggies will camp out here while Operation Switch plays out. You and I have pull-out couches in our offices, and many of the froggies do as well. Those who don't, have camp beds. It's not going to be much fun, and there'll be long periods of boredom as we wait for something to happen, but this is just too important to not give it twenty-four seven attention."

Silvia nodded. "I agree. Food?"

"I've asked Annette to handle that. Limited menu, but it'll have to do."

Silvia laughed. "No fantastic French wines, then?"

"No. In fact, I'm not going to drink much until the last of the replacements is in place."

She laughed. "God. Marginal food and limited booze? You must be really stressed."

He laughed, too. "Let's check out the systems."

The conference room had war room functionality built in, but this was the first time it had been used for such a complex mission. There were four large screens, each programmed for one of the Gang of Four countries.

Silvia seemed calm, but Alan knew her well and saw that she was on tenterhooks.

She spoke calmly. "Are we sure that all the replacements are one hundred percent committed and are ready to take the leadership positions?"

"Yes," Alan replied. "The one with a specific role in the assassination is clear on what he needs to do.

Those who'll step in after the assassinations also know the timetable and what is expected of them."

Silvia had been standing, but now sat down at the head of the conference room table. "Okay. We changed the roll-out and Russia is now the first. We'll meet here in the conference room at 10:30 a.m. Jason is aware of the schedule. Who is delivering the vodka to Menklov?"

"Angkasa."

"We'll update Jason at the various milestones and pray he doesn't get impatient and wants to interfere."

"Amen to that."

Chapter Nineteen

Menklov sat in his living room looking down at a roaring fire which, combined with the superior central heating, kept his dacha warm even as winter played out its last snowfalls.

He was expecting a visitor, and at the appointed time, his aide entered and announced that a young woman had arrived.

"Have Yuri search her and bring her in."

After ten minutes, Menklov's bodyguard brought the woman into the living room. She wore a COVID mask, but it revealed enough of her face for Menklov to observe that she was Southern Asian. Perhaps Indonesian or Filipino.

He had been informed that the messenger did not speak Russian, so he asked her in English, "You have a package for me, yes?"

"Yes."

She offered a long, thin cardboard box, which Menklov opened cautiously. Inside was a bottle.

Silvia received a call from Tina late in the morning.

The CIA director sounded tired. "We have early warning that Russia is probably about to launch one or more hypersonic nukes on Ukraine. Are you close to implementing your plan, whatever it is?"

Silvia held her breath. They were close, but if anything went wrong, they would not have a way of stopping the missile launch. She had not shared the mission details with the CIA, and was not prepared to do so now.

"We have an action in play," she answered. "Let's hope it works and works in time."

At about 10:40 a.m., Alan received a call. It was from Angkasa in Moscow, where it was 5:38 p.m. He picked up and triggered the speaker option. The voice spoke distinctly but briefly. "Our man has the vodka and is setting off."

"Thanks." He hung up and turned to Silvia. "So, Menklov is on his way to Chekov and the Russian president should be facing the entrance to Hades in a couple of hours."

She regarded her coffee cup, but left it in its saucer on the table. "We just wait now."

Both knew what would happen next, but Alan spelled it out again. "The protocol is that if the president dies, the head of the FSB is the first to be notified. Ching has bugged the man's personal phone. When he gets the call, we will know."

"What if whoever finds him doesn't make that call? Or he uses a different number?"

"Worst case, the Russian news agency will report it."

"And the prime minister?"

"Still in Iran."

It was 6:00 pm in Moscow, and Chekov sat at his desk assessing his battle strategy for Global Strike. He had briefed his prime minister on the plan before he left for Tehran, but other than this man, Chekov had kept Global Strike to himself.

The plan was detailed and comprised a dozen orders, which he had constructed with the help of his aides and several of the senior military commanders. Each commander operated in isolation on what Chekov had described as a scenario exercise. None believed that their part would ever be implemented. The risk of an international conflict was just too great.

However, missiles with tactical nukes had been armed and could be launched immediately by a single order from the president.

It was February 20. Yang and he had discussed the plan earlier that day. Chekov was ready to give the order that would launch the initial attack. He sat back, looking at the red phone on his desk, and knew that he only needed to pick it up, speak his directive, and four hypersonic missiles with nuclear warheads would be fired into the night sky towards Kyiv.

In two hours, he would make the call which would launch Global Strike.

Next to the red phone was another, this one yellow. It was the one he would use to call Yang and inform him when the missiles were launched.

He looked at the schedule for the other countries. Two days later, Iran would launch a larger, long-range missile with a cluster of warheads, which would penetrate Israel's Iron Dome and destroy Tel Aviv. A week after the Iranian launch, Kim would send four ICBMs to the United States. These would be shot down by American ground-based interceptors from the Alaskan airbase at Fort Greely, but it would occupy the attention of the American military and its citizens as Russia and Iran continued their attacks.

As he thought through the strategy, he knew that Yang would wait until March 1 for his attack, when the West would be focusing on the Russian, Iranian, and North Korean threats. *I know he's using us as a diversion, but it accomplishes my goal, so why not?*

He looked at his watch.

Recently, the stress of the economic issues in Russia, the sanctions, the lies he was telling, and the daily disappointments as the war in Ukraine encountered headwinds had pummeled that man, and he had resorted to the habit of most of his predecessors: drinking copious quantities of vodka.

There was a sharp knock at his door and he shouted out, "Enter."

A military guard entered, followed by a man he knew well, Boris Menklov.

"Mr. President, it's so good to see you again," the man said. They embraced, but Chekov raised an eyebrow at the guard. The soldier nodded that the visitor had been searched for possible weapons and was clean.

"Sit down, Boris. Something to drink?"

"Actually, I have brought with me a special vodka, which comes from Latvia and has subtle flavors of lavender and juniper. Let me open it and we can toast your recent successes in Ukraine."

Chekov showed his suspicion and examined the bottle the oligarch had shown him. He checked that it was still sealed.

"One moment."

He reached for his desk phone and spoke a few words into it. A short time later, his door opened and the same guard entered with a thin man who was pale and looked sickly.

"My friend here will sample the vodka first," the Russian president said, glaring at the man, then at the bottle.

"Mr. President, I am not trying to poison you." Menklov's expression showed surprise.

"Of course not. But I have received threats on my life and I cannot take chances."

"I understand."

Chekov looked at the man who had been convicted of crimes against the state and now was a designated food and drink taster. "Open it and pour yourself a glass."

"Yes, sir."

The man did so, and when the president nodded, he swilled back the vodka.

Chekov watched him for any reaction and the man let out a small smile. "It's very good, sir."

"Go."

The taster left with the guard and Chekov poured two glasses, one for himself and one for Menklov. They both drank and then Menklov's smartphone alerted him to an incoming message.

He looked at it and said, "It's a text. A fire at one of the mines. I need to go. I am sorry we did not have longer. I wanted to hear all your great stories about the latest on the special military operation."

As he was leaving, the oligarch turned to the president, who was settling down in an armchair.

"Enjoy the vodka."

Three hours later, the guard heard the president's yellow phone ringing, but it went unanswered. He was concerned and entered the room.

Dimitri Chekov, president of the Russian Federation, lay slumped in his chair with an expression of pain on his face and his eyes wide open. It was obvious that he was dead, but the guard confirmed this by checking his pulse.

The guard looked around the office, but did not focus on the nearly empty bottle of vodka. The yellow phone stopped ringing.

As his protocol dictated, he left the room, locked the door behind him, and placed a call to the personal phone of the head of the FSB.

The director of the bureau was about to settle down to a late dinner with his wife when it came in. He called for his car and started to decide on actions that would limit the chaos in the aftermath of the president's death. A call to the prime minister, who was in Tehran, went unanswered.

As he was driven to his office, he made calls and put measures in place to prevent armed conflicts by supporters and detractors of the late president. He advised the local police that the FSB was in charge of the incident.

Almost as an afterthought, the FSB director instructed an aide to have the Kremlin's doctor examine Chekov's body. A thought passed through him. *The guard said he was dead. Let's hope he's right after all this.* He paused. *I wonder if it was from natural causes or something else. Well, the medical examiner will know.*

At 2:00 p.m., Ching knocked on the door of the Purple Frog conference room. Before Silvia could say, "Come in," he rushed into the room. He was clearly excited.

"And?" Alan asked.

"We got him. The telephone lines in the Kremlin are all lit up and the person in charge of security did call the FSB director and told him that Chekov was dead."

"Cause of death?"

"The Kremlin doctor just confirmed a heart attack. Natural causes."

Alan, though elated by the news, kept a serious face and stated," One down, three to go."

Silvia exhaled. "We've started it. Let's hope we can finish it."

She made a call to Jason.

"Russia Phase One is complete. Now we'll see if the switch works."

Jason spoke slowly. "Congratulations." Then he let out a sigh. "I know you don't want me interfering, but it's torture just sitting here waiting for your updates. There must be some other way."

"No, Jason, there isn't. At least you have good weather down there. Even though Alan and I have been in a warm conference room without windows, there's snow on the ground and we can hear sleet beating on the roof. It's supposed to ease up later this week. But you need to stay calm. Alan and I have everything under control. Have a rum cocktail and celebrate that we have started with a win."

"Hmph."

Chapter Twenty

In the war room in the Beijing presidential palace, a senior aide held up the phone and shook his head. "The bastard is not answering?" Yang asked. The aide shook his head again.

The Chinese president looked up at the screens about the room and focused on the one piped in from China's earth satellite systems. By now, he expected it to show the missiles exploding over Kyiv, but they showed nothing. Calls to Chekov had not been answered.

"Fucking Russian. Probably drunk and has forgotten the schedule." He spoke to the empty space about him and remembered that he had ten of his senior generals waiting outside the room. He had summoned them for a major meeting in which he would reveal the Global Strike strategy.

He motioned to his aide and instructed him to contact the Russian president using whatever means necessary.

Fifteen minutes later, the man approached him, shaking. He was clearly concerned about the news he was about to deliver.

"My source in the Kremlin says that President Chekov has…"

"Has what?"

"Has died, sir."

"Died? He is dead?"

"That is what I am told."

"How did he die?"

"It has all the signs of a heart attack, sir."

"So, who's in charge now?"

"The prime minister, I suppose. But he is in Iran attending a factory inspection. Shall I contact him?"

"I wonder if he even knows about Global…"

"Knows about what, sir?"

"Never mind. Let me think about this. Follow up with the Russians. I want confirmation that it was a death by natural causes and not something else."

Yang needed time to process this change of events. *Global Strike cannot go ahead as planned. Or could it? If Iran destroys Tel Aviv and Kim launches on the United States, this is probably all the diversion I need.*

"Have the generals come in."

After they finished their call with Jason, Silvia and Alan sat silent for a minute or two. Silvia asked, "What are the next steps in Russia?"

"I'll talk with Menklov, if I can reach him. I expect he is quite busy rounding up Chekov's allies and implementing the power grab we worked out with him. We have a number of assets over there who don't know about Switch, but will be aware of what's happening. I need intel on how it plays out."

Silvia looked at her empty coffee cup. "The second set of assassinations will be tomorrow, in Iran. Is everything still in place?"

"Yes. We're as ready as we'll ever be."

A convoy of army vehicles threaded its way across the sparse landscape north of Tehran, towards a location close to the border with Turkey. In addition to the armored personal carriers and other military vehicles, there were three Aurus Senat limousines. These had been purchased from Russia and were styled after the Rolls Royce. They were armor-plated. The Supreme Leader, Ayatollah Jannali, and his president, Farid Moradi, were driven in the last one of these, a random placement to provide confusion to anyone targeting the powerful Iranians. Both traveled in the same vehicle; the other two limousines were empty decoys.

The Russian prime minister rode in the limousine with the two Iranian leaders on the way to the factory, where he would review the latest improvement in the drones being fabricated. In the preparatory stage of Global Strike, Iran had agreed to supply the new generation of drones to Russia in exchange for a nuclear delivery missile.

The leaders had planned to travel to the facility by helicopter, but intelligence had hinted at a possible attack by Israelis using surface-to-air missiles to kill the Iranians in the air. Considering this, they opted for a motorcade rather than the vulnerable aircraft.

As the convoy progressed, fighter aircraft flew overhead, providing additional protection for these men who had feared for their lives for years.

The Supreme Leader sat, his mind switching between thoughts of God and thoughts of the Global Strike that, after several months of planning, was within twenty-four hours of implementation.

Teaming up with the Chinese, Koreans, and Russians was anathema to him. However, joining this unholy liaison would allow the furtherance of his goals for a more powerful Iran and the destruction of Israel. Russia had provided a delivery vehicle two months before, and the Chinese technical staff had helped develop the warhead which would be used.

Iran's own uranium refinement resources had already delivered weapons-grade material in sufficient quantity to make the final steps straightforward.

Boda Morozov, the Russian prime minister, was next in line to the Russian president, and he sat uncomfortably with the two Iranians. He did not speak Farsi, and there was no interpreter present, so Moradi and Morozov conversed in French. Each spoke English better than French, but they had decided that using French was preferable to accepting the dominance of English as a popular, worldwide language. The Ayatollah, when he spoke with the Russian at all, used his somewhat limited French.

For most of the trip, the Iranians spoke with each other in Farsi, and the Russian was annoyed by what he regarded as rudeness on their part. Then a call came through to his smartphone with a distinctive ringtone.

"Excuse me. This call must be urgent."

He answered it in Russian and listened, asking a few brief questions as he heard the news. "Oh, my God. Why didn't you tell me sooner?" The Russian paused as he listened to the answer. "Oh, I turned my phone off last night." Neither of the Iranians understood what was being said, but could tell from the Russian's expression that something was amiss.

The Russian prime minister commanded his caller to text him a detailed report. He hung up and looked absently out of the limousine window before looking back at the Iranians. "Supreme Leader," he said to the Ayatollah, "I have important and terrible news."

Moradi snapped," Just tell us."

The Russian leaned forward as his phone started to display a stream of text. He considered this for a moment, then said, "Dimitri Chekov has been found dead." The cleric and president gasped and Morozov continued, "It was a heart attack."

Moradi glared at the man. "Not an assassination?"

"No. My people say that it was from natural causes. A heart attack."

The Supreme Leader hissed at the man. "Did he launch the missiles? You know it was the first act in Global Strike. Find out if he did so before he…" He didn't finish his sentence.

The Russian looked down at his phone and read the text. "No missiles were launched."

Moradi let out a string of expletives in Farsi and the Ayatollah harangued him. "Blasphemy is unacceptable, even now." The Supreme Leader then asked his president, "What do we do now, Farid?"

"We've come too far to back out. The Russians were just going to create a diversion. We have the missile and the warhead. I believe we should stick to the plan."

The cleric nodded. "Death to the Jews."

The Iranian president switched back to French. "Please accept the condolences of the Iranian people. The Supreme Leader has decided that we shall continue the assault on Israel and the West."

Boda Morozov, now default President of the Russian Federation, said, "I must get back to Russia. The country needs me now. I'll get Global Strike back on track."

The Ayatollah leaned forward and said, "You are here to inspect the factory. After that, we'll have a helicopter fly you back across the Caspian Sea to the Russian border for your return trip to Moscow."

A short time later, the convoy arrived without mishap at the drone factory, which was several hundred kilometers from another secret underground facility. This was currently home to a long-range missile, the RS-28 Sarma, a recently completed Russian program which carried ten multiple independently targetable reentry vehicles. The projectile and its payload would shortly be set to a ready state and await an electronic order to fire it.

On this trip, the Iranian president, as always, had with him the equivalent of the U.S. nuclear football. He planned to use it after the drone factory inspection to unleash Iran's attack on Israel. He and the Ayatollah would be well away from the launch site, so if anything went wrong, they would be out of harm's way. In addition—though unlikely—if the Israelis, or perhaps the United States, launched a retaliatory attack on Tehran, they would still be safely away from the city. The man who for the last half hour had been the new President of Russia would also be safe and on his journey back to the Russian capital.

A small band played as the important visitors left the motorcade surrounded by security guards and overshadowed by snipers on the surrounding roofs. The elite Quds troops provided solid protection for the Iranian leaders and their Russian visitor.

The general manager of the factory greeted the entourage, and he bowed low to the Ayatollah. About one hundred engineers and technicians had been assembled to greet the party from Tehran, and the general manager waved his arms for them to bow deeply in front of their religious leader.

Several were beckoned forward and introduced to the visitors.

A short time later, as the group moved into the factory, they saw a young man before them. The general manager gestured to the man. "Supreme Leader, allow me to introduce you to Abin Jafari. Jafari is one of Iran's young engineers who has worked extensively on the new generation of drones."

The general manager did not know that Jafari was known as Iran #46 to his contact in Purple Frog. The man bowed to the cleric and the politicians.

The engineer showed enthusiasm as he gestured for the visitors to follow him. "Let me show you what we have. It is really exciting."

The party followed the young man through the building and came to a large area in which about five hundred drones were stacked on racks around the perimeter. Troops with submachine guns at the ready accompanied the group.

One drone was on a stand in the middle of the room and the group was escorted over to it.

Morozov, who now regarded himself as the new Russian president, spoke. "Show us how this works."

Abin Jafari knew that if he said aloud what was on his mind, the guards would either arrest him immediately or kill him.

He wanted to tell them that God was not a warrior wanting to kill even his own believers if they believed different aspects of the faith. God was kind. God was merciful.

Instead, he turned and opened a compartment on the drone, reached inside, and placed his hand on a switch he had installed that morning.

"Go with God," he said.

The explosion killed all in the room, including the Ayatollah, his president, and Boda Morozov, President-elect of the Russian Federation. It also killed Jafari.

The switch was connected to a small radio transmitter, and a message was relayed to Alan Harlan in Virginia before the detonation destroyed most of the drone facility.

Alan's laptop registered the message and he sighed. It meant that this part of their plan had been completed. The two Iranian leaders were now probably dead, as was the Russian prime minister, who would have fought Menklov for the presidency. It meant that Abin Jafari had given his life to support their goal.

Alan had mixed feelings. He knew that both Russia and Iran had lost their current leaders and Global Strike was severely damaged. However, the death of Jafari filled him with remorse mixed with pride in the young man who had come up with the idea to make the kill. He had given his life for the good of his people and the world. Any doubts Alan Harlan had hidden at the back of his mind were now gone. Purple Frog would succeed in this mission to prevent a third world war.

Ten minutes later, Ching had hacked into radio transmissions from the drone factory and one of Purple Frog's Farsi translators confirmed the deaths and the partial destruction of the facility.

But Alan's job was not done. He reached for his phone, called his best Farsi simultaneous translator, and asked her to set up a call with the cleric next in line to become Supreme Leader.

When Alan spoke, he did not mince words. "Ayatollah Beheshti, you will know by now that Iran is in need of a new Supreme Leader, and you are next in line for the role. You will be offered it, but you will not accept it."

After the cleric heard the Farsi translation, he shouted a string of words, and continued doing so until Alan had his interpreter interrupt him.

"Jannali's death is being called an accident, but you probably don't believe that. The next leader could also meet with an accident. Do you want to die?"

The ayatollah was silent and Alan continued.

"We have significant evidence that ties you to your wife's death. As well, we know of your other acts against her. We can, and will, expose this evidence to the Assembly of Experts and the media if you are tempted to accept the appointment. When offered the role, you will say that ill health prevents you from taking the position and that you wish Ayatollah

Motahari to be chosen instead. You'll endorse him to be appointed Supreme Leader."

After a string of words, during which the female interpreter's eyes widened, shocked at the language coming from the mouth of a holy man, the cleric calmed himself and asked for time to consider the offer.

"You have one hour," Alan said. "Please don't attempt anything foolish."

An hour later, Beheshti grudgingly accepted the pact.

Alan next called Ayatollah Motahari. The man was expecting the call and stood ready to take the role of Supreme Leader. He would accept the position and announce that his predecessor was killed, perhaps by God's will, in a tragic accident when inspecting a factory in northern Iran. He would decree seven days of public mourning and also announce a new president, a man who was also well aware of the assassination plot.

Chapter Twenty-One

The populous of North Korea worshiped President Kim Ji-yoo as a god, but there were factions in the government and the military who would be delighted by his death. Kim knew that he had no real friends.

When his father died and Kim took over, he was immediately besieged by most of the current hierarchy, who wished his approval and to retain, or improve, their positions. Many saw the change as allowing them to settle old scores and advance their careers.

Even before his father's demise, Kim had developed a network of internal spies, and on taking power, was able to decide whom to trust and whom not. He managed to resist a collapse of his newly acquired kingdom, promoted some, and removed others. Those not in favor were sent for "re-education," or, in most cases, jailed or executed. Kim ruled by the stick and not the carrot.

His sister, Kim Jyong-sook, was largely unknown. She displayed intellect and strength and supported her brother's decisions, particularly those which required violence of some kind. But did her goals reach higher than being just the president's sister? He had never appointed her as his deputy, but she had quietly taken that role. Although she supported her brother completely, he suspected that she harbored ambitions beyond being the number two player.

On February 21, Kim and his sister met in a room in the presidential palace, which had a dozen large screens and news feeds from many of the worldwide news agencies. Today, the world press would be reporting on a new offensive undertaken by Russia, so the president and his sister sat together watching a bank of television sets, each tuned to a different international news channel. Simultaneous translators were present standing by to provide the stories which would unfurl in these foreign languages.

Kim looked at his Patek Philippe wristwatch, smiled, and motioned to his sister, who also checked the time. The Russians would have already launched their strike, and at any moment the story would break.

Kim had called for a bottle of French champagne, Dom Perignon. The pair stood with glasses in hand, waiting to toast the start of the war. Each news channel displayed a different set of stories and the translators provided a Korean summary of each. A strike of railway workers in the United Kingdom, a

U.S. senator accused of taking bribes, a shooting in Tel Aviv, post-Christmas celebrations in Kyiv. No missile strikes were reported.

Kim was agitated, and his sister even more so.

She snarled. "What is happening? Have we been double-crossed? This is Yang's work, I guarantee. You should never have trusted that Chinese crook."

Rossiya, the Russian state television network, displayed a "Breaking News" banner.

"Ha. Here we go."

The screen showed the exterior of the Kremlin and a reporter commenting on something which seemed of great importance. Kim smiled, thinking they were about to announce the attack. His Russian interpreter translated the story.

"Sir, President Chekov has died of heart failure."

Kim Ji-yoo hastened to his office and instructed an aide to place a call to Yang. The man attempted to do so, but then turned to the North Korean president and said, "Sir, President Yang's office refused the call."

Kim screamed at the man and thought, *Perhaps Yang is grappling with the impact of Chekov's death, or he is implementing some plan of his own.*

Either way, Global Strike was not going to be implemented on schedule.

Kim returned to the hall where his sister was still watching the news programs and the various spins put on them by the different country agencies.

"What's happening, brother?"

"I don't know. Yang is not responding."

"Should we be worried?"

"I don't know."

Then another station flashed a breaking news banner. It was Namayesh TV in Tehran.

"They're a little late. Rossiya reported Chekov's death an hour ago."

Kim's Farsi interpreter provided the Korean translation. It was not what he expected.

"A terrible accident at a factory north of Tehran claimed the lives of the Supreme Leader, the president, and also the prime minister of Russia, who was visiting…"

Kim's sister swore and hurled her champagne glass at the television set.

———∞———

A few hours later, Kim's sister asked, "Shall we skip Namp'o?"

"No. These deaths are probably not coincidental, so leaving Pyongyang and being surrounded by a thousand military loyalists might be safer."

They had planned the trip to Namp'o Shipyard Complex to launch a new attack destroyer and had specifically chosen February 22 for the event.

The launch of the destroyer would include the Western tradition of breaking a bottle of champagne across its bow as it was released to slide down into the sea. The shipyard's management had debated the situation for many weeks, and they faced a major choice. If they made the wrong decision, the principals might be imprisoned, or worse. Finally, they'd made the call. They would use a Korean sparkling wine rather than a more expensive, and less accessible, French champagne.

Kim's sister shook her head, her short hair bobbing back and forth. "How secure will we be getting there?"

"We were going by motorcade, but given the circumstances, we'll change that. Helicopters. One for you and one for me. And a few decoys in case someone tries to shoot us down. I'll arrange a fighter escort, too."

"It'll take us about half an hour, so we need to leave here at three. I have a meeting with Hwang Jang Yop to discuss the economy before then. He'll be careful with his requests, but I know he thinks the economy is more important than the military. He is always pushing for farm subsidies rather than our nuclear program. When we get back from the shipyard, let's think about him. Maybe he needs some re-education."

Just outside Pyongyang, a passerby would have noticed the truck, which seemed to have broken down on the main highway, its hood open and two poorly dressed Koreans fiddling with the engine. The cell phone of one of them rang and he took the call.

"Damn," he said. "It's the airport. Kim and his sister are taking helicopters to Namp-o. We won't be needed today."

They closed the hood and re-entered the vehicle, which started on their first attempt.

"What about the rocket launchers?"

"We'll take them back to where we had them stored. Maybe Kim will return by road and we can finish this."

Alan looked at his watch. "We should have heard about North Korea by now."

Silvia glanced at him. "Is there a problem?"

"I'm not sure. Our intel, courtesy of our friends in Langley, says that Kim and his sister are traveling to Namp'o, and our asset was in place on the main highway." His phone rang and he picked up. Then he covered the mouthpiece and said to Silvia, "It's Korea."

He returned to listening to the message.

After a moment, he said, "Bummer. Is Plan B still a possibility?"

He listened again and his boss grew impatient to know what was going on.

At last Alan hung up. "Kim switched his trip to Namp'o. He's going by helicopter."

"So?"

"The ambush obviously won't work, but we have a backup plan. Neither plan was foolproof, but fingers crossed that this one works."

The five helicopters were closely guarded, and a maintenance crew was undertaking the final checks on each. Outwardly they looked like one another, but two had luxurious interiors while the other three concealed heavy machine guns.

A Korean of medium height and a uniform like the other maintenance crew advanced to the first of the two VIP craft and opened a compartment near the engine facility. He identified the rubber tube which fed fuel from the tank to the engine and wrapped a cloth he had brought with him around the tube. He carefully released a vial hidden in the cloth, which allowed an acid solution to come into contact with the fuel line. He repeated the action on the second VIP helicopter.

"Hey, you," an armed security guard called to him. "What are you doing there?"

"Just checking the fuel pump. We've had some minor issues which could slow their flight, so I wanted to make sure everything was all right."

"And?"

"Everything is fine."

"Good. Now get away from the aircraft."

"Certainly, sir."

Just after 3:00 P.M., the five helicopters rose into the sky above the maintenance field and flew to a yard at the back of the palace. It was bitterly cold, with a temperature of 20°F, and Kim and his sister wore heavy snow jackets as they crunched across the forecourt to board. Aides helped the pair enter their craft, and shortly afterward, the helicopters flew into the gray sky.

Six minutes later, as they proceeded over the low hills south of the capital, the engines of each VIP helicopter spluttered and cut out. The pilots tried to restart them, but without success, and the aircraft, out of control, crashed into the hillside.

Alan received a call from the South Korean "maintenance" worker who had heard over his radio about the crashes.

"Three down, Silvia. I need to make some calls."

Hwang Jang Yop, the Minister of the Economy, announced the death of the leader and his sister an hour later, before any search parties had even reached the site.

He declared emphatically that the leader's eleven-year-old son, who was safe in Pyongyang, would become supreme leader and that he, Hwang, would be the regent who would shepherd the boy and advise him on the political and military decisions that needed to be made. He strongly hinted that the focus on spending would shift from the military to the domestic economy.

Chapter Twenty-Two

Alan and Silvia and many of the froggies were exhausted. They had stayed awake for most of the first intensive week, taking short spells for sleep. As well as orchestrating the assassinations, placing the new presidents into their positions required extensive work, including hacking into email accounts and personnel files, social media trolling, and faked leaks about potential rivals. However, the initial actions of Operation Switch had succeeded, and the few hiccups they encountered were addressed and dealt with.

The news of Kim and his sister's deaths was confirmed and the Purple Frog replacement, Hwang, seemed to have successfully stepped in.

They called Jason and provided him with an update.

"The Russian, Iranian, and North Korean hits have been successful. We just have Yang to go."

"How are our replacements working out, Alan?" Jason asked.

"Menklov ran into significant opposition, as we expected, but he seems to be coping. His previous links to the army and the FSB are holding well, and while he's not a shoo-in at the moment, he's leading the other contenders. The 'accident 'in Iran that took out the Russian prime minister within a day of Chekov's demise raised some eyebrows, but Menklov is showing an even more ruthless streak than we imagined."

"Is Angkasa out of Russia yet?" Jason asked.

Alan sighed. "Not yet. She's still in a safe house in Moscow, but will be taking a train to Cherkeesk and be on the Turkish border in a few days. So far, so good."

"And Iran?"

"Beheshti went to the Assembly of Experts, declined the supreme role, and recommended Motahari. The Assembly agreed."

Silvia gave a short laugh. "Now, let's hope China goes as well."

Yang was furious. If even one of the other leaders had died or been displaced, Global Strike was at risk. Now three of them had. The Iranian and Korean deaths were classified by those countries as accidents, and the Russian president had, allegedly, died of a heart attack. He laughed.

When he'd learned English, a skill he did not boast about but which gave him a significant advantage in negotiations with the West, Yang had read the full set of James Bond books by Ian Fleming. He recalled a particular phrase in Goldfinger.

Once is happenstance. Twice is coincidence. The third time, it's enemy action.

He paced about his office, thinking about the turn of events. *They know about Global Strike. The West knows, and they're fighting back.*

An aide entered the room excitedly. "President Yang, planning for the parade is complete. This will be an even bigger festival than in 2019 for the seventieth anniversary."

Yang hesitated. If he was right and the three deaths of the others in the Gang of Four were indeed an enemy action, his life was likely at risk as well. Attending the parade would be dangerous. However, to cancel it, or not attend, would be a negative for his standing among the Chinese elites.

The president turned to his aide. "It is important that we display our full military might." The Chinese president smiled as he sat in his favorite armchair in his office in Beijing.

After the man left, Yang called in his head of security.

"I am concerned about threats at the parade. I must be protected against any attempts on my life, or against the party members who will also be attending."

The head of security expected the president to question him about this and had prepared his answers. "A company of your personal troops will be guarding you and the members. Surrounding all will be a glass-clad polycarbonate screen, one hundred and fifty feet of it all around the dais. Ten feet tall. Totally transparent, but it can withstand any projectile short of an anti-tank missile."

He continued specifying the helicopters and drones that would patrol overhead, the snipers on the rooftops, and the cordoning of the area.

Yang nodded, but he was still worried.

The reviewing dais was located in Tiananmen Square in the center of Beijing and could be seen from the top floor of a new building nearly a mile away across the city. The building, tall and slender, had been named by its architect 'the Needle.'

Yang's personal guard oversaw security for the parade and was well aware of the building and its position relative to the reviewing stand. Over a thousand office workers went there daily as they labored on administrative duties from early morning until the evening. The looming parade changed that. Guards cordoned off the building a week before the parade and refused admittance.

A contingent of troops searched it thoroughly and then sealed it. After that, they posted sentries, but otherwise did not believe it necessary to re-enter the establishment. While sound, this approach allowed anyone who could avoid the sentries and gain access to have unlimited passage anywhere in the facility.

All the publicity pictures of Yang depicted him in a dark Western suit and tie. To the outside world, he projected the image of a civilian and a businessman. The day of the parade would be different. It was time to show the world that he was, at heart, a soldier. An officer. Commander-in-chief of the People's Liberation Army.

The president commissioned a major Chinese fashion designer to develop his custom uniform for the parade, and Yang regarded himself in a full-length mirror before leaving for Tiananmen. The uniform had been made in dark red silk, which reflected his position and his embrace of China's military strength. The style pleased him.

While being dressed, an aide delivered a message, which arrived from an agent in Moscow. It confirmed Chekov's death by natural causes.

Yang frowned. "Check it out again. I don't like coincidences."

He turned his mind to the parade. His planned speech would set the tone for a renewed expansion of China into territories outside its current footprint. He would not mention Taiwan by name, but the implication would be obvious. He would not mention Japan. His military attire positioned the president clearly as China's supreme commander.

The gang that Betty had led for many years held the man who had been her lover and then her husband in great reverence. By avenging her death, Abdul now enjoyed their full support for his attempt on the Chinese president's life.

As with all major cities, a warren of tunnels for rail transportation, power, communications, services, and sewers ran under Beijing. Abdul's gang knew the layouts well, since they used the network to distribute various illegal contraband.

Three days prior to the parade, they followed their maps to the Needle through the sewer system and carefully took down a wall that led into the building's basement. With the building closed, the gang had free reign within it. They put the wall back, but in a way that it could be opened in a few minutes.

Early on the day of the parade, they dismantled the wall, and two hours before the parade was due to start, Abdul entered the Needle basement carrying his M107 long-range sniper rifle. He was accompanied by three men who carried a large case.

The party made its way to the top floor of the building and Abdul scaled a small ladder to reach the roof area. From here, he would have a clear shot even though his target would be a mile away. The men joined him on the roof and quickly erected special tarpaulins, which blended in with the surface of the roof and would hide them from any patrolling helicopters or drones. Under one of these, Abdul set up a few instruments which would test the wind, temperature, humidity, and other environmental factors which might affect his shot. He then positioned his rifle on its bipod and loaded it with a magazine of ten armor-piercing rounds.

On the floor below, his helpers opened the case and withdrew a large, heavy weapon, which they carried up to the roof and placed under a second tarpaulin.

The assassin lay behind his weapon and the larger weapon was about six feet away.

Abdul looked over at it. It was a Missile Moyene Portee, or MMP, a French fifth-generation anti-tank missile launcher. One man sighted the tube on its tripod and loaded a single missile.

"Ready, sir."

They waited as helicopters and drones passed overhead and the parade started. A group of ICBMs was driven past Yang's dais and Abdul observed them through his telescopic sight.

He did not need to hurry, since the parade would last for at least another hour before the speeches commenced.

Abdul slid over to the MMP and checked that the man had sighted it correctly. It was a fire-and-forget device, and when the trigger was depressed, the missile used its laser sight to follow a path directly to its target. Abdul's man just needed to squeeze the trigger. He confirmed that Yang, as expected, stood on the dais behind the protective screen, which spread across it.

As he lay on the roof of the building and sighted his rifle at the reviewing stand, he thought back to when he had first encountered the mysterious, clandestine organization that he now knew as Purple Frog.

Abdul's mission in Brussels was to assassinate the new head of the European Union with a long-range shot similar to the one he was about to use in Beijing. For many years before and since, his signature trademark had been for rifle shots from about a mile away, which most security operations did not see as possible. They often did not check vantage points from which such a shot could be taken. In the Brussels project, he had been tricked into aborting the attempt.

In the distance, he heard the faint sound of bands in the parade and took up his position with his rifle. He put on ear protection and turned to the man manning the MMP. "Fire it."

The man squeezed the trigger and the missile left the tube, speeding at nearly a thousand miles per hour.

It sped towards the bullet-proof glass wall, but veered away from the center of the dais.

Through his telescopic sight, Abdul watched the reactions of the people assembled on the review platform. Several bodyguards saw the missile's incoming flight and immediately reacted, pulling the president to safety.

The missile missed where Yang was standing by about thirty feet and exploded, tearing a hole in the bullet-proof shield. No one was hurt, and the people on the platform, though frozen in fear, showed their relief that the perceived attempt to kill had been averted. Even if the shield had been destroyed in front of the Chinese president, his bodyguards had already pulled him to the ground and covered him with their bodies. A rifle shot would not have been successful.

Yang rose to his feet and the bodyguards joined him. Through his sight, Abdul could see him clearly.

The president, although shocked by the attack, was jubilant that the missile had missed and he had not been harmed. He stood, no doubt feeling confident, since the protective shield still stood between him and any would-be assassin.

Then, as Abdul had planned, a crack appeared in the protective shield as the polycarbonate that had been struck by the blast vibrated. The entire wall fell to the ground. His protection was gone.

As it fell, Yang's face twisted into a look of disbelief. Abdul squeezed the trigger. The single shot killed the Chinese president, hitting him in the chest and tearing out his ceramic body armor and most of his upper body.

The police and military security reacted immediately, but by the time they'd determined from where the shot had likely been fired, Abdul and his assistants had made their escape through the underground tunnels.

Within an hour, Premier Huang Wei, who was on the reviewing stand, assured the Chinese population that the perpetrators would soon be caught and punished. In the meantime, he would lead the country.

Alan put down his phone and looked at Silvia. They were alone in the conference room.

"That was Abdul confirming the news reports. Yang is dead. Huang has taken control. We got 'em all."

Over the previous two weeks, the stress of their situation had resulted in Silvia maintaining a fixed, serious expression on her face. Now she smiled, and, picking up her phone, called Jason.

"Got 'em all," she said. "Each of the Gang of Four is dead."

Jason's voice came over the speaker. "My God. That's great news. And the replacements?"

"So far so good. Let's hope they won't be a disaster."

She spoke to her intercom and requested that Bob Famosa—the head of profiling—Ching Tong, and Donna Strickland join them in the conference room.

She reached into a cabinet, withdrew various bottles, and poured each a glass of their preferred alcohol. She congratulated each of them.

Her mind was still attempting to cope with the enormity of what they had just done. They had changed the world order. *I just hope it's a positive move, that it does not backfire.*

Silvia drank a glass of Sauvignon Blanc in one gulp, and the others also swilled back their drinks.

"I needed that," she said. "We've all been on tenterhooks for the past two weeks and haven't left the office. I don't know about you, but I have been totally stressed out. Thank you everyone for your dedication."

The room became silent. Donna at last broke the quiet. "Thank God you had showers installed here when you set up the company, Silvia. Otherwise, life would have been unbearable."

Silvia poured herself another glass of wine. "None of you have been drinking much over the last couple of weeks. Professional. But it's over for now, so drink up, and then go home. Alan has a skeleton crew on duty here, so if there are any major traumas, we'll each be notified. Eat some real food and get some real sleep."

Alan called Jess.

"I've been watching the news reports, darling. Congratulations."

"Thanks." His reply was short, but she could read the pride in his voice.

"I'll bet you have hardly slept and have been eating junk food. Are you coming home now?"

"In a half hour or so. I just need to finish up a few things."

"I know you are the real chef in our household, but, you may remember, I make a great paella. Shall I start prepping that?"

"Other than sleeping, I can't think of anything better." She heard him laughing. "Well, one thing."

The following day, Silvia spoke to the Chinese premier. "Mr. President, I'm calling to remind you of the deal we have." Huang Wei was delighted by the new title Silvia used to address him.

The next week, several dozen officials and members of China's parliament were arrested. The military commanders pledged their support for the new president, who ordered a stand down on the exercises close to Taiwan.

A week later, a driver collected Abdul at Penang Airport and drove him to his estate. Tears ran down his face as he remembered Betty and their time together. He now faced a solitary life ahead. Perhaps he would return to his life as an assassin until that life caught up with him.

As the SUV pulled up to the front door of his house, a spectacularly attractive young Chinese woman came out to greet him.

"Good afternoon, Mr. Johnson, sir," she said. "I am Ling Lau. A year ago, my cousin, Betty, instructed me to comfort you in the event of her death. Here I am."

Chapter Twenty-Three

Over the next few days, Ching Tong set up communication links with each of the newly ensconced heads of state. He used audio connections rather than video, and it was routed through a series of relays which made sure that no one could trace its origin nor eavesdrop on the calls.

Alan looked up from his laptop. "Call coming up with Iran, Silvia."

"Thanks."

When it connected, she started the conversation.

"Good evening, Mr. President, and congratulations on your new role." She spoke into a microphone in English and a froggie simultaneous translator interpreted her words into Farsi. Voice modification software ensured that the recipient of the call would be unaware that a woman was speaking with him.

The new Iranian president barked into the phone," Who are you people? What do you want of me?"

"We've covered this before. You and the Supreme Leader were briefed before your predecessors were removed, and you have now taken Moradi's place. We have indisputable proof of your role in the takeover and what you are calling the 'accident' at the drone factory. We fully intend to use that if we need to."

"So, do you work for the American president?"

"No. We are independent."

Silvia had been through all this previously with the man, and he was now sounding like a worn record. She knew she needed to repeat what she had told him weeks before, but resented having to do so. "Our objective is simple: we will do whatever is necessary to foster peace in the world. We would love to insist that you change some of your domestic agenda, but we'll resist asking for that."

She paused as the interpreter caught up.

"We only ask that you de-escalate Iran's plans for war. You will cease the development of nuclear weaponry, you will allow international inspectors to verify this, and you will halt the manufacture of drones. You'll disable the Russian missiles." She imagined the new president bristling and repeated, "We shall not interfere with your policies within Iran. Is that clear?"

The president's voice slowed as he spoke precisely so that the interpreter would convey his message accurately. "When we talked before the unfortunate accident that happened in the drone factory, we agreed to these terms. Ayatollah Motahari is a moderate and was uncomfortable with the venomous approach of his predecessor against other Muslims. Attacking Israel made no sense other than for spite and power. When you negotiated your arrangement with him, he appointed me to replace Moradi. We accept the situation."

She nodded, though he couldn't see her. "Good. Now, let's work on a schedule for your actions that will lead to the outcome we both agreed on. Remember, this must be kept secret. If you allow others to know about our arrangement, they will exploit it to your disadvantage."

"You may not like me very much, but I am not a stupid man."

Silvia and Alan held similar follow-up calls with the new president in Russia, the mentor of the boy ruler of North Korea, and the premier, now president, of China. North Korea and China were now run by individuals who wanted to develop their domestic economies rather than spend resources on their military, and this made the discussions easier.

One discussion with the new Russian president was more difficult than the others, and Silvia and Alan left the call with concerns about their choice.

Alan summed it up. "I don't like it. He said the right things, but I have the impression that we can't trust our little oligarch. He's too used to having his own way, and was evasive when we wanted dates for the troop withdrawals from Ukraine. We can expect treachery from all four countries, but my bet is that Russia will be the first to display it."

After a busy day, Silvia looked up from her computer and her eyes traveled around her office. The room was not large—about fifteen by fifteen feet—and her desk buttressed one wall. Other furniture comprised a desk chair and two visitor chairs, and there was also a two-seater couch, two armchairs, and a small coffee table.

It was late, and although tired, she experienced the adrenaline boost which came from the caffeinated beverage, but also from her new position. World power. She now held leverage over all of the major U.S. enemies, and could, and would, issue commands that they would follow. Her head spun at the magnitude of her role.

While Jason held the ultimate power in their new world, Silvia held the reins on a day-to-day basis.

Alan still joked about her title of Galactic Princess, and though she laughed the first time he used the term, she now faced the reality of her position.

The headiness swirled, and then a moment of self-doubt flooded over her. How could this woman of just forty-seven years be more powerful than the president of the United States? Her mind took in the enormity as she considered the situation.

I need a drink.

She rose from her chair and walked a little unsteadily to a corner bar area, selecting a bottle of Sauvignon Blanc from the small refrigerator. She paused and returned it. Instead, she took a whisky glass, added a single cube of ice, and was about to pour some Talisker Storm, Alan Harlan's favorite single malt Scotch. She spotted the bottle of Dark Storm that Jason had given Alan some months before, which they had not finished on their flight from St. Croix. *Dark Storm is what we have just fought and won.* She poured herself a healthy measure.

She intended to sip the golden liquid, but found she wanted to take a gulp, so she did so. It burned her throat and she regretted her impulsiveness. She coughed a little, but the alcohol was doing its job and she felt more relaxed. Dropping into one of the armchairs, the one she always used, she swirled the Scotch around its glass and then took a sip. *Better.*

Looking up at a large screen on her wall, she took in the organization charts showing the relationships of the new players who were now installed across the globe.

After a moment, she picked up a wireless keyboard and accessed a checklist of actions. Each would be implemented in the next week or two, and the result would be a significantly more stable world, with so many of the recent threats to peace eliminated.

You done good, Silvia Lewis. But thank God that Jason really holds the power.

Alan broke the spell by knocking on her door and entering. He had recovered from the exhaustion he'd experienced as they'd rolled out Operation Switch, but still looked tired.

"Have you seen the latest media reports?" he asked.

Silvia looked up. "Yes. The deaths of the leaders and the ascent of their replacements have made prime time for days now."

"There have been a lot of purges and reorganizations, but our new leaders seem to be well entrenched. The press also indicate a significant de-escalation of military operations. None of the journalists have started to weave stories about the coincidences, but these will come sooner or later and will probably be dismissed as fake. Conspiracy theories."

"You pulled it off, Alan. You should be a happy man." Silvia offered him the Talisker bottle." Drink?"

"Not tonight. I'm going home early. And you ought to do the same."

"I know that look, Alan Harlan. You're on a high, and you deserve to be. I guess you and Jess will continue the celebration."

"We'll certainly be doing something, but I'm not sure you would describe it as celebrating."

He called Jess at work and suggested she return to their apartment earlier than normal.

Jess was proud of her husband, and had been for years, but now more so than ever. He had taken risks, acted, and accomplished the impossible. She knew he would continue to be excited, and she felt a burning desire to run her fingers over his body. She realized that she wanted him. Needed him. Now. Making love had always been good. Actually, very good, and tonight it would be better than ever.

Fred Shidler was a television celebrity. For many years, he produced a television show, *Business 2.0*, in which he interviewed key leaders of industry, and the success of the show led the network to offer him an additional program, *Government 2.0*. On this program, he questioned senior members of government both in the U.S. and in other countries.

On an evening in late-March, his guest was the head of the United Nations.

"Good evening, Mr. Secretary," he said, "and welcome to *Government 2.0*."

After several general interest questions to allow his guest to relax, Shidler raised the hottest issue of the moment.

"The events of the last few weeks have been incredible. The United Nations has been operating for nearly eighty years with a charter to foster peace across the world, and with respect, sir, the organization has not achieved a lot."

The Secretary-General gave a watery smile and presented a rehearsed speech on the achievements of the international body, but Shidler had made his point to his TV audience.

He continued the interview. "Some people have said that the structure of the UN is flawed. One example is that Russia can become head of the Security Council even after invading another sovereign country."

The Secretary-General anticipated this rebuke and said, "There are many things wrong with the organization, but without it, the world would be worse off. Even though we argue and debate and deal with the protocols and vetoes, we still have a vehicle for communication. Without it, there would be more anarchy across the planet."

I've got you on the defensive now, so on to the next point Shidler thought.

"A month ago, we faced the possibility of a world war. But now there have been major breakthroughs. Russia has agreed to leave Ukraine, and Iran says it will stop nuclear development. North Korea has also agreed to do so, and China is talking about recognizing Taiwan. They even said they might be pulling out of the South China Sea. These are monumental changes. What role did the UN play in this?"

The Secretary-General was silent. He had a prepared answer for this question indicating a larger involvement by the UN than he knew was the case. But he shrugged. "I would like to take credit for these events, but I cannot. It is a mystery to me, my staff, and the delegates. But let us thank God for this, whatever your religion."

Chapter Twenty-Four

In Moscow, even as Shidler interviewed the head of the United Nations, Boris Menklov was ecstatic. Chekov, a man he had come to hate, was dead. His predecessor's prime minister had died just one a day later in a mysterious accident in Iran, and Menklov was certain this was not a coincidence.

The oligarch had moved rapidly and secured the backing of Russia's senior generals and the FSB, who agreed that Boris would be named the next president of the Russian Federation. A purge of Chekov's allies had started, and certain members of the armed forces and the FSB identified as potential threats were being dealt with.

Working with Chekov over the years had provided billions of dollars of wealth for Menklov, but taking the top job now allowed him to make tens of billions more.

His thoughts turned to the mysterious organization that had enabled his rise to power. They had demanded payment—withdrawal from Ukraine.

Boris knew that this made sense. Chekov was stupid to have started his crazy operation, and it had proven to be his undoing. The invasion was a disaster, but Chekov's pride had stopped him from admitting defeat and withdrawing his troops. He also held a valid concern that withdrawal would be perceived as a weakness. Important allies might turn against him.

Menklov pointed to the mistake that his predecessor had made, and at least in the interim, called for the evacuation. He would plead with the West to lift the sanctions that were strangling the Russian economy.

What his mysterious benefactor was demanding made sense, but the idea of this foreign agency holding him to ransom was anathema to him. He would play along with their demands but instigate an investigation, find out who they were, where they were located, and remove the threat. Then he would rule as he wanted, not as a puppet for some Western organization.

He remembered the South Asian woman who had delivered the bottle of vodka to him. His external security cameras held a picture of her without her mask, and he would use this to trace her.

I wonder if she has left Russia already. Probably, but maybe not.

Looking down at a list of names, people who would be arrested or killed in the next few days, he pushed it to one side and reached for his phone.

"Colonel Lomonosov, I have an urgent task for you. There is someone I want you to find for me."

Angkasa Foyle was one of Donna Strickland's newer recruits, and while her temperament was improving, she suffered from a need for independence and delighted in breaking the rules Purple Frog had put in place. The escape plan from Russia called for her to stay hidden for several weeks in a safe house in Moscow before taking a train to the south and then crossing into Turkey.

Donna had warned her to keep her face covered, feigning fear of COVID and wearing a face mask, but Angkasa hated the mask and decided not to wear it other than when she actually met Menklov. Thus, the security cameras in the oligarch's dacha picked up a clear image of her face as she entered and left.

Colonel Lomonosov arrived at the FSB headquarters in Lubyanka Square, and thought about the resources he needed for his mission.

Sophisticated facial recognition software was installed across Russia, and the FSB colonel turned to this to locate the Asian woman whom he had been tasked to find.

A junior FSB technical officer was tasked with finding her. He downloaded the identified camera image, ran it through a program that broke it down into a series of parameters, and then used these to search cameras in real time across much of the Federation.

"Do you have a location, corporal?" Colonel Lomonosov asked.

"Not yet, sir. She's not visible to any of the cameras at present. Let me access some of the historic data." An hour later, he called out," I've found her. Or I know where she was."

"Tell me," the colonel said, sounding excited.

"She boarded a train from Moscow for the south a day ago."

"South? Where?"

"The train terminates at Nasran, near the border with Turkey."

"Can we get to her?"

"Yes. It's a slow train, with stops everywhere. We could fly people down and board at Cherkeesk."

His superior nodded. "The president was very clear. We need her alive. We need information from her. She might have a suicide pill. I don't even know who she is. She might even have colleagues with her. The president told me nothing."

He picked up a phone.

"Send Olga to Cherkeesk by helicopter. She is to meet the train headed for Nasran and join our little Asian woman on board."

The woman was middle-aged, and displayed a charming smile when she sat down in the third-class railway carriage next to the Indonesian Australian. As the train jolted and left the station, she started to speak Russian, but Angkasa interrupted her. "I do not speak Russian. I am a student from Djakarta. I am in Russia to study."

The woman switched to English and they began a conversation.

"What are you studying, dear?"

"Art."

Angkasa was suspicious, but the older woman seemed harmless. She laughed and joked and Angkasa felt relaxed. She was within a few miles of the Turkish border, and her forged papers would pass as she left the Russian Federation and entered the NATO country.

"Are your studies focusing on a particular artist? Or is your research general?" the woman asked.

Angkasa shared the names of three specific Russian artists and delivered her rehearsed speech on how they were regarded as important on the international stage.

"They are of great interest in Indonesia, where we strive to keep on good terms with the Russian Federation."

The woman started to reach into a carrier bag she carried and Angkasa stiffened, but the woman withdrew a bag of candies and offered one to the Asian woman, who refused it.

Then, as the train rocked, the woman appeared to lose her balance a little and spilled the candies across the floor of the train compartment. Angkasa's gaze shifted to them and did not see the woman withdraw a small syringe. She felt a prick in her arm, then turned with a look of astonishment.

The Purple Frog field operative glared. "You bitch."

The woman smiled as Angkasa's eyes became blurred and she fell into unconsciousness.

The cells in Lefortovo Prison in Moscow had thick walls, and prisoners often thought they were the only ones held in the facility. In most prisons, the screams of men and women being tortured instilled fear in the other inmates listening from their cells. In Lefortovo, this was not the case, but the silence throughout the prison added to its ominous threat.

The interrogation cells witnessed many savage inquisitions, usually brutal attacks by sadists who liked to inflict pain. Normally, the aim was to extract a confession, and the methods they used achieved this goal even if the inmate was not guilty.

"I have just the man for you, colonel," a senior prison administrator said, greeting the FSB colonel. "He'll have her talking in no time."

"I do not want some illiterate thug harming my prisoner. I am a sophisticated man, and my primary objective is to find out the location of a clandestine spy group of which this woman is a member."

Colonel Lomonosov smiled at the man.

"I shall use my own methods. When I succeed, I will be rewarded. But if I fail, I will be punished. Perhaps even at the hands of the goon you are offering me."

The deputy threw up his hands, acknowledging the colonel's rank. "We have her in interrogation cell twelve. Follow me."

She sat on a chair, her hands secured to a fixed bolt in the metal table in front of her. The colonel entered the cell and sat opposite. He signaled the prison administrator to leave them.

He carried a briefcase and opened it slowly, withdrawing a folder. He placed it on the table and made a show of reading it.

After a few minutes, he looked up and quietly asked in perfect English, "What is your name? We're going to spend a lot of time together, so it would be easier if you told me that, at least."

"You can call me Helen."

"I see. That is the name on your passport. It's a very good forgery, but it *is* a forgery."

She did not reply.

"You know that you will never leave here alive, don't you?"

"I'm a student. I want to speak with the Indonesian Embassy."

The colonel laughed. "I have people in this facility who want to hurt you. They believe in the old-fashioned way of interrogation. Beatings, removing fingernails, electric shocks, and, since you are a pretty little thing, they will definitely rape you while you are still relatively unharmed."

She grunted. "Fuck off."

"But I have found that information given under torture is often false information. Purposeful lies, or invented just to have the pain stop. I have a different way. Do you want to hear about it?"

She said nothing.

"Over the past couple of years, I have used a team of scientists to work in a more efficient approach. A truth serum."

Her eyes widened.

"People have been trying to develop such a drug for decades, without success. My team has not perfected one, but we are close."

He sat back in his chair.

"Traditionally, the drugs administered are scopolamine or sodium amytal and sodium pentothal, and my people have mixed a cocktail of these and some other barbiturates. It's not perfect, but it worked well in trials. I believe it will be effective."

She remained silent.

He smiled at her. "President Menklov has not told me much, other than you work for a spy organization in the United States. He has a few specific questions he needs answered."

Her eyes widened further as he continued.

"Oh, there's one problem. My cocktail has a side effect. The drugs allow only a half hour of questioning before the subject dies."

Chapter Twenty-Five

Tish Richey brought her ArmaLite AR-15 to her shoulder and fired two rounds. Each found the center of the target, which was set two hundred yards away. She then threw the switch that converted the rifle to fully automatic and released a burst of five bullets, which followed the earlier two into the target.

She was bored. It was a quiet time, and several of the people she referred to as her "associates" had returned to their homes, some in other states. Typically, she enjoyed some downtime between what she referred to as" gigs," but this time the team had been idle for nearly a month. She and the rest of them needed some action.

A voice called to her from the house. "Hey, Tish. You got a message."

"Thank you, God," she said, and walked across the yard to the back door of her Indiana home. The house was spacious and old, and had been owned by a large family when times were better for soybean farmers. When the farm had failed, the bank had foreclosed and sold it to Tish for a few thousand dollars, and the fields around it made excellent training grounds. She and her associates were able to shoot off their guns without any interference from neighbors.

One of the rooms on the ground level of the house was set up as an office, and the young man who had called to her pointed to her laptop, which displayed a pop-up indicating the receipt of an encrypted message. She saw that it was from a contact in Russia.

She had undertaken a dozen operations for the Russians, and these had started small, planting sensors or eavesdropping devices in government buildings and in the electric grid. However, recently, they had been commissioned to make a series of attacks on local organizations in neighboring states. Her Russian contact had not told her the reason for these operations, but she assumed they were to focus law enforcement attention on white supremacist groups. The Russians seemed pleased with what she had accomplished, but they were stingy. They often wanted something complex, but were not willing to pay much.

Still, with nothing else on the horizon, something was better than nothing. She read the message. It was brief and spelled out a mission different than those she was used to, but well within the capabilities of her and her associates.

They were to locate a building in northern Virginia, attack it, and kill all the occupants. The brief said there were about seventy people at the site, but less than a dozen would be armed and trained to fight.

She shook her head. The projects she and her people undertook nearly always held risks, and in a few cases, ended up in a shoot-out with private contractors or law enforcement. This project, however, involved killing civilians. She was about to send a reply indicating that she was not prepared to undertake the project when her second-in-command strutted into her office. He was tall, good-looking in a "bad boy" style, wore a long beard, and was heavily set.

"Hi, Tish. What's up?"

She looked him up and down and took in his arrogance. But he was handsome, and they had great sex together.

"Russia wants us to take out a civilian facility in Virginia."

"Great."

"Not great, idiot. We're soldiers, not murderers."

"Hey. We don't got nothing else on now, and the Ruskies sometimes pay well. How much are they offerin'?"

She told him the figure and he whistled.

"They sure want them suckers dead."

"We're not going to do it, Snarly." She called him by a nickname that the man had used for several years, based on one of his most common traits.

"Come on, Tish. Why the fuck not? If we don't do them, the Ruskies will find someone else. The result'll be the same, but someone else gonna get the money."

"No. We aren't doing it."

Snarly approached her, took her head in his hands, and kissed her on the neck. He started to run his hands over her body.

"Not going to work, Snarly." But she let out a sigh and kissed him back.

"You know you want to do it."

"No. I don't."

"Let me convince you."

A half-hour later, she was dressing and said, "Let me find out some more details from the Russians. It may be that it's a military target after all."

———∞———

Later that week, Tish decided to undertake the project. Snarly had been persuasive.

She mentally thumbed through the resources she had at her disposal. There were thirty-two of them. Most were men, but she also had a half dozen women who had seen combat in the Middle East with U.S.

forces. They were all battle-hardened, and would be eager to test out their skills again.

She set up some calls with her Russian contact at the FSB, who filled in answers to most of her questions. She still had mixed feelings about the project as she learned more about their target.

On the one hand, she was pleased to find out that this was a private organization. She would not be taking on a part of the FBI, CIA, or any other official law enforcement agency. To do so would unleash a nationwide search with unlimited resources that would undoubtedly lead to their capture, or worse.

The target was alleged to be the only location of this private group, which meant that, providing they killed them all, they could expect no retaliation.

On the other hand, being private, it was not a military target and comprised civilians. Her conscience raised its head again, but her mind shifted to the thrill that would come from the operation and the sex she would have afterwards with Snarly. Also, this time, the Russians had not been stingy with their agreed payment. She shrugged off any doubts she still had.

She agreed on a timetable with her FSB contact and summoned her lieutenants for a briefing.

The FSB had been vague about the building and its occupants. They knew its address and the number of occupants, but had limited intel on the security measures in place.

"We'll just play it by ear," she said to Snarly.

Jason Overly hated the title, but he was now known by the froggies and their management—and the Advisory Board—as the Galactic Emperor. Throughout his career managing Avanch, he had focused on meeting goals, not on acquiring power for its own sake. Now, he held the world in his hands. He could, if he wished, push his puppet leaders to do things that would be in his interests alone.

As he thought of this possibility, he laughed out loud. This was not Jason Overly. Jason wanted world peace, and certainly was not interested in being emperor. *Maybe that's what'll make me a good and benevolent dictator,* he thought.

He sat on a stool at his bar in Sugar Ridge. Doris slid behind the mahogany counter.

"Jason, you lookin 'radiant tonight. What can I get you?"

"In the last week, I and others have saved the world."

"Doris rolled her eyes. "Sure, sure. Now, what you want to drink?"

"What is the best champagne we have that's chilled?"

"I don't know champagne, but you always seem to like the Tattinger. That we got cold. That do you?"

"Perfect."

She found the bottle and showed off her skills by removing the foil and the cage, then popping the cork quietly under pressure so as not to allow a drop to spill.

"You see? You taught me well." She laughed and poured him a glass.

"I'm celebrating tonight. Please join me in a glass."

"You know I'm not a drinker, but maybe just one."

She poured a half glass, raised it to her mouth, and drank.

"Damn good," she said.

"What do you have for dinner tonight?"

"I got two terrific steaks from Hans. I'm gonna grill them Pittsburgh rare, just as you like 'em."

"Two?"

"Probably too much for just you?"

"Join me?"

"I'm not into beef, and we've had a relationship for ten years, which I am not going to change. I cook, you eat."

She placed her half-empty glass of champagne down and looked at him. A grin invaded her face. "Why don't you call your friend, Ben? I would be amazed if he didn't like steak, being an Australian and all."

"Great idea." Jason picked up his smartphone.

An hour later, the entrance intercom sounded and Doris opened the gate for Ben.

"G'day." He beamed as she opened the front doors to welcome him to the pool deck. He smiled at her and gave her a big hug.

"You behave yo'self," she said, laughing.

"Hi, Ben." Jason said.

"G'day, Jason."

They went to the bar.

"What will you be drinking, sir?" Doris loved flirting with the man.

"Cut the 'sir 'bit. And you know that already. But more important, how about a really expensive cocktail?"

Jason answered for her. "We have lots of that here. So choose your poison."

"I'm not a connoisseur like you, but I like Scotch."

"One of my best colleagues likes Talisker best. I have a Talisker Storm and a Dark Storm. From the Isle of Skye, and a salty taste for the sea."

"Right up my alley."

Doris poured him a Dark Storm.

"Ice?"

"Dunno. What do you think, Jason?"

"Alan takes just a single cube."

"Sounds good to me."

Doris added the ice cube and the two men toasted each other and sipped their drinks.

"I got the coals on so you can eat soon," Doris said. "How you like your steak, Ben? Jason, he likes it Pittsburgh rare."

"Pittsburgh rare. That's burnt on the outside and rare at the center, right?"

"That's it."

"Fan-bloody-tastic."

A half hour later, they sat outside in the dining pavilion enjoying the local beef.

"This is a beaut, Jason. Thanks for inviting me." Ben smiled at his host. "You look happy. Do you have something to celebrate?"

"I do. But I can't tell you about it."

"Spoilsport. Anyway, we should celebrate the news over the past few weeks. Four assholes are dead, and the new guys seem to want a more peaceful world. Let's celebrate that, eh? Cheers."

Jason laughed at the irony of Ben's toast and raised his glass.

As they were finishing the meal, Ben raised another issue. "How's it going with the nightmares? Still having them, or is that a thing of the past?"

"I still have them. Actually, it's really one dream, which I used to have every week or so, but now it's every night. I still can't recall any details, but I have this image of blood. Lots of blood." He finished his steak and said, "I have to fly up to Virginia first thing tomorrow, so let's go to the bar, have an Armagnac, and call it a night."

"Sounds good to me."

Ben looked up at the sky as they walked across the pool deck.

"Looks like rain."

Chapter Twenty-Six

That night, Jason experienced the nightmare again. He woke with a premonition that something bad was going to happen, and soon. He rolled over and sank back into a troubled sleep. Outside, a tropical shower poured rain onto the pool deck and roof.

It was overcast in the morning, but Jason still rose early, swam a few laps, and dressed for his trip north. An hour later, he was flying at thirty thousand feet, looking out the small window of his Cessna Longitude.

The pilot announced, "Mr. Overly, we are heading into an area of turbulence. Please make sure your seatbelt is securely fastened."

The image of blood from his dream returned and he closed his eyes, trying hard to remember the details of the nightmare. He was unsuccessful.

Some hours later, Jason's limousine entered the car park at the back of the restaurant in northern Virginia and came to a halt beside the battered SUV. Jason alighted, dashed through the wet car park, and entered the older vehicle for the final part of his journey to the Purple Frog offices.

As they drove through the rural countryside, Jason reflected on what they had achieved. There had been a couple of hiccups, but they had pulled off Operation Switch across the four axis countries. He should have been elated, but at the back of his mind, the darkness returned.

It was still raining lightly as the SUV passed through the gate to the Purple Frog building. Jason did not see a group of men and a few women, who wore camouflage clothes, lying on the ground within eyesight of the building.

The SUV entered the parking garage and Jason alighted. He walked the steps up to the door leading to the main entrance, passed the reception, and entered the office area, passing various cubicles and offices before joining Alan and Silvia in the conference room.

Jason took the espresso that Alan handed him. "Where do we stand, Silvia?" he asked.

"Menklov has been inaugurated and has ordered his troops out of Ukraine. They've negotiated with the Ukrainians and there will be a cease-fire while the Russians complete their withdrawal."

Jason sipped the dark brew. "Excellent. Any news on Angkasa?"

Silvia shook her head. "No. We've not heard anything from her."

"She should have made it out of Russia days ago," Alan said. "I'm afraid we must assume that she's dead or captured. If she's been captured, we must assume they'll break her."

Silvia sighed. "We should relocate our HQ. In the interim, I've made a lot of changes to our security protocols."

Jason nodded. "I agree with making a move. And we have the funds from the batteries operation with November Swan to pay for it." He looked over at Alan, who looked tired. "Keeping you up, Alan?"

"No. I didn't sleep well. A nightmare. Vague, but very bloody."

Their conversation was interrupted by an alarm bell.

Jason looked around. "What's that? Fire?"

Silvia put down her coffee cup. "That's security." Her phone rang and she picked up. She listened for a minute, then hung up. "We have people moving towards us. The security cameras indicate there are about twenty or thirty of them, and they're armed with assault rifles and a few heavier weapons."

Silvia entered a few commands on her laptop and the screens about the conference room displayed the security camera feeds. They confirmed the assessment made by Purple Frog's head of security. It was clear that an attack on Purple Frog was about to be launched.

Jason's eyes opened wide. "Who is it? And how the hell did they know where we are?"

Alan and Silvia answered him together. "Angkasa."

Silvia triggered the "Call all stations" intercom and announced, "Listen closely. We will shortly be under armed attack. Follow the procedure. Protocol three. Good luck all."

Purple Frog had five armed security guards, and Donna's four field operations people were also in the building, but matched against the force of thirty coming in, the odds were poor.

However, all the froggies had been recently trained in the use of firearms and had weapons in their desks. They had trained rigorously on what each should do in the face of an attack. Donna, her team, and the guards took up positions on the main floor and the others hastened down the stairs to the basement. Silvia, Alan, and Jason remained in the conference room and watched the images from security cameras. The incoming attackers were well deployed and moved cautiously through the short grass of the field outside the building. It was clear they were experienced and well-disciplined. The well-hidden cameras picked up the faces of the intruders, and it was easy to locate their leader.

Alan stated the obvious. "It's a woman."

The woman's face showed surprise, probably wondering why there had been no defensive fire yet. Perhaps she was unsure that they had come to the right location.

Jason pointed. "Look at camera seven."

An image from the back of the building indicated that a small party had been deployed there and had taken up position with a heavy machine gun, no doubt to fire on people attempting to escape through the rear.

Tish signaled for her team at the front of the building to advance and they did so, slowly scanning the area for potential threats. When they reached the front doors, they checked them and found them locked. Tish signaled for explosive charges to be attached, and less than a minute later, there was a short, muffled blast and the doors were blown open.

With the exception of the small group that she had sent to cover the possible rear escape route, Tish mustered the bulk of her force, to enter. All her troops wore protective body armor with helmets and face guards. Each carried an AR-15, which had been modified to allow fully automatic firing. Their guns were loaded with thirty-round magazines.

She looked at the entrance to the Purple Frog building, peering through the smoke from blowing off the door, and directed three of her men to advance to the gap and move inside. When they did so, they were hit by a fuselage of handgun fire from inside. While the body armor saved their lives, two were injured.

Tish waved a command for a second assault, and this time, a group of six fought their way inside and sought cover in the interior hallway.

"Snarly, secure the entrance."

"Roger that." He moved forward, firing at where he thought the defenders might be positioned. No one returned fire and he signaled for others to join the first group in the reception area.

A fusillade of bullets peppered Tish's associates and three more fell, injured. Snarly and his men returned fire.

"Tish, they only got handguns!" he shouted. "This is going to be easy pickin's."

The firefight continued and the attackers gained ground, breaking into the main office complex.

A number of rounds was fired at them and Tish recognized the sound of a new weapon, an M16. Four of her troops, including a woman, were hit in the face with high-velocity bullets, which shattered their face guards and killed them. A blonde woman had taken the shots through an aperture in the wall of one of the offices.

Tish's force saw that the office area comprised rows of cubicles, which were surrounded by offices, meeting rooms, and a large conference room. The area seemed empty, with the exception of the glass-walled conference room, in which three people huddled together around a bank of computer monitors.

"Ha. Sitting ducks." Tish aimed her rifle and let off a burst of four rounds. They hit the conference room walls and made small indents, but did not shatter the glass.

"Fuck. Bulletproof."

Apertures opened in several of the offices and more barrels of M16s emerged. These fired into Tish's troops and killed five more of her associates.

Snarly looked about the office area and saw there were only a few defenders firing on them. No others were in sight. "Where are the rest of these fuckers? We counted about seventy going in this morning."

Tish let off four shots and then called to Snarly. "This is a single-story building. There must be a basement." She pointed. "Steps there. Take ten men.

They're civilians, so should be a cinch. I'll sort out the security guys up here."

It became clear to Tish that the conference room, while looking to be an easy target, was impregnable to rifle fire.

"Explosives. Bring that glass wall down!" she shouted to one of her men. He removed a slab of explosive and advanced to the pockmarked glass of the conference room. Then a bullet from someone outside the conference room hammered into the back of his helmet and, although not killed, he dropped like a stone, knocked unconscious.

Others associates attempting the same maneuver were also shot, and Tish saw that her team was starting to lose this phase of the battle.

Snarly led ten men down the stairs to the basement area and was surprised at the layout. There was a firing range and a series of miniature buildings.

"What the fuck is this?" he exclaimed.

From a window in one of the closest buildings, a rifle appeared briefly and fired two shots. Two more of Tish's troops fell as the bullets tore into their heads.

Donna Strickland had descended—with two of her team—through a back staircase and was ready to stop the attackers from harming the lesser-skilled froggies. She saw that the froggies had spread out as their protocol directed. Most had handguns and knew how to use them, but they were not experienced in fighting, and would have qualms about wounding or killing their attackers, despite knowing that the interlopers would kill them given half a chance.

She slid down from the window behind the solid concrete of the building as Snarly's people directed their fire towards her. Then she crawled to another aperture and repeated her earlier attack, killing two more of the attacking force.

Snarly was mad. "The blonde was upstairs. How the fuck did she get down here?"

He waved his hand, ordering his troops to retreat, but as they did so, several were caught on the stairs by two men shooting down from the floor above. Snarly could see these defenders—one an African American and the other Caucasian—were highly skilled. More of his troops died. He left the fight and returned to the basement area.

Upstairs, Tish still had half of her troops uninjured, but saw that what she had expected to be a simple mission was turning out badly. Another three guards from the facility ambushed some of her men, and they were killed before they could determine the location of their enemy and fire on them.

The fight lasted less than twenty minutes, and it was clear to both sides that the defenders had the advantage.

Chapter Twenty-Seven

In the basement, Snarly had avoided being killed along with his fellows and had located two of the froggies, a junior hacker and a member of the translation team. They raised their guns as he advanced on them, but did not have the instinct to shoot and kill. He put a burst of bullets into each and they fell dead to the floor.

A bullet from another froggie wounded him in the arm, but the pain only made him angrier. His face mask had clouded over and he tore it off.

Then he broke cover, running forward with his AR-15 blazing. One of the defenders, whom Snarly took to b Chinese, held a Glock, sighted it, and squeezed his trigger. The 9mm round flew straight into Snarly's forehead and killed him instantly.

Upstairs, Jason, Silvia, and Alan stood in the conference room, well aware of the battle going on beyond the glass wall before them. They could see the attackers being gunned down by the Purple Frog security guards, but then one broke through and ran to the glass wall, holding a block of plastic explosive, ready to adhere it to the glass. All three instinctively ducked, but the man faltered and blood spewed from his head.

Alan looked out at the dead attacker and his mind flashed back to his nightmare of blood that the attacker's destroyed face displayed.

Two of Donna's field operations men, Kemal and Paul, left the skirmish and exited the building through the front door. They circled the facility and spent less than two minutes disposing of the small team at the back, who were there to cover any attempted escape. Then they returned to the main battle, which was winding down.

Tish and six people in her team were all that was left of the attacking force, and she realized that her people could not win the fight nor be able to escape. It was also clear that the people they had attacked had suffered several casualties, and probably a few deaths, and giving up would likely result in painful retribution. She decided that she and her troops would fight to the end and die a soldier's death, if that was their destiny. But she wanted to take a few more of the defenders to their deaths with her, so she called out to her troops.

"Enough. We'll give up. Do you understand me?" The defenders heard her words, not realizing they were a code to have her people feign a surrender.

The attackers laid down their rifles and the Purple Frog defenders, led by Donna Strickland, emerged to take them into custody.

Donna shook her head. "What do we do with bloody prisoners?"

Seeing their attackers surrender, Jason marched past Silvia and left the conference room. She called to him to wait, but, as always, he thought he knew best.

The attackers' leader gave a signal and her troops pulled out handguns and blasted away at the advancing froggies. Kemal took a bullet in the arm, but Donna, wary of the surrender, let off a burst of fire. The others supporting her did the same.

The leader's people were all killed, but she was only wounded. She slumped to the floor, dropped her Glock, and raised her hands.

"You can get up now, Jason," Silvia said. He had leapt out of the way and dropped to the floor as the leader had started her final battle. He was moving slowly, as if in pain.

"Are you all right?" Silvia asked.

Alan emerged from the conference room and saw a large stain of blood on Jason's suit jacket.

"Oh, God. He's been hit."

All the froggies had been trained in first aid, and several were further trained as medics. One rushed over to help.

He looked at the wound, his face showing that it was serious.

He turned to Alan. "We need to get an ambulance. Should I call 911?"

Jason had closed his eyes, but now opened them and said in a weak voice, "No. Silvia, you need to keep this whole operation secret."

The medic shook his head and she said, "If we don't get an ambulance now, you're going to die."

Jason gave a short laugh, which cut off, clearly causing him intense pain. "I'm going to die anyway." He turned to the medic. "That's right, isn't it?"

The medic hesitated, then said, "That's right, sir."

Jason closed his eyes, and when he reopened them, he looked back and forth between Silvia and Alan. "I don't feel like I have much time, so let me cut the small talk."

He spoke softly but firmly.

"I'm so proud of you two and the froggies. Twelve years ago, I developed a plan to bring, at least, a pause in warfare around the world, and you made my dream come true. I gave you an impossible mission and you pulled it off. Your next phase will be to keep the new assholes in check."

His expression showed the pain he was feeling as he looked directly at Silvia.

"We joked about calling you 'Galactic Princess.' Now, you are about to be promoted. You'll need to be strong and ruthless. You're dealing with the scum of the earth, and we have put some of them into positions of extreme power. You will need to act as a dictator. A tyrant. But you'll be a benevolent tyrant, and that's what will make the difference. This is my final bow, and I want to give you your new title: Galactic Empress."

He laughed, but the pain expressed itself, changing his laughter to a cough as blood flowed from his mouth. His eyes glazed over and he looked sightlessly into space.

The medic checked his pulse and shook his head.

"Smartass to the end," Silvia said quietly as tears rolled down her face.

Silvia turned to the leader of the attackers. "Alan, gun."

He knew what she wanted it for and what she was about to do. "Are you sure you want to do this?"

She nodded and Alan checked that the Glock he held had a round chambered, but the safety applied. He handed the weapon to his boss.

Silvia let out a cry that sounded like a wounded animal and walked over to the woman, who was shaking with what she knew would happen next.

Silvia pointed the handgun at her, released the safety, and fired a single round into her head. The woman's expression changed to one of calm.

Silvia and her husband, Brian, sat in their living room. Brian glanced at his wife, who was holding back tears. It had not been difficult for him to pick up on her state of mind.

He was an intelligent man, and although Silvia had always spun him the line that she ran a small division of a software company, he was aware that she did something more than that. She never talked about her work, and he had periods of feeling helpless as she obviously struggled with some emotional issues, but she was not prepared to share her pain with him.

"Are you okay, darling?" he asked.

"Actually, the answer is no. I am not okay."

"Can I help? Can't we, just for once, tackle this bogie together?"

He held her in his arms. Ordinarily this would be a prelude to them making love, but not now.

"Jason was killed today."

Brian knew she worked for Jason Overly and had often harbored a suspicion that they were more than just boss and subordinate. On the few occasions he'd expressed his concerns, Silvia had laughed and assured him it was only a work relationship. He believed her.

"How did it happen?"

She hesitated, clearly trying to decide how much she should share.

They had been in love for nearly thirty years, and she had supported him when his hedge fund had gone belly up. However, she had always kept things from him. She sighed, clearly making up her mind to change that. "He was shot."

"Shot? As in shot with a gun?"

"Yes. And we had two others of our staff killed — a translator and one of our junior hackers."

"Hackers?"

Silvia was now openly crying. "We killed all the attackers. I killed their leader."

"You did what?"

She stopped crying, dried her eyes, and looked at him.

"I shot her in the head."

"Good God."

She gave him a small smile and said, "I'm going to tell you all about it. About Purple Frog. About what I have been doing over the past twelve years."

Shock spread over his face.

Her smile widened. "Then, my darling, I'll need a release. I need you to make love to me. How would you like to have sex with the most powerful woman in the world?"

The next day, Silvia looked out through the pockmarked walls of the conference room into the cubicle area, which was largely destroyed from the hail of bullets from the attackers. She called a meeting with Alan and Donna.

It was the day after the attack, and Donna settled down on the couch in the conference room. Alan sat in one of the armchairs.

"We lost two froggies and another three were wounded, but not seriously," she said. "And then there was Jason." She squeezed her eyes shut as she thought of their late boss. "He was a pain in the ass at times, but he was a great friend and a great leader."

"How did his girls take it?" Alan asked.

Silvia let out a groan. "It was the hardest call I have ever made. Both of his daughters loved him totally, and I had to tell them a story that was not the whole truth. In fact, nowhere near the truth. I think they suspected there was something more to the story, but didn't press it."

She sipped from a glass of water in front of her.

"Our friendly doctor in St. Croix will write up the death and we'll avoid an autopsy. The funeral is the day after tomorrow in St. Croix. Jason wanted his ashes scattered on the waters down there."

Alan looked over at Donna. "I've organized his jet. Silvia and I will take the body down tomorrow. Anil, Avanch's CEO, is ferrying his girls and their families from the West Coast."

"It would have been appropriate for most of the froggies to be there, especially you, Donna," Silvia said, "but we have to keep Purple Frog in the shadows. In the meantime, find out who was behind this."

"Understood."

Chapter Twenty-Eight

They flew down to St. Croix in Jason's executive jet, conscious that in the cabin with them was a coffin containing his remains.

When they arrived at the private aircraft area, the coffin was transferred to a van, which Jason's local bodyguard drove to a doctor, who wrote the death certificate, shaking his head.

"Last time I did this, it was for another man, Darnell. He worked for Jason and was a good man. I knew him, and I knew if Jason wanted his death logged as natural causes, he had a good reason. No problem."

He looked down at the body of the technology billionaire, which showed an obvious gunshot wound in the chest.

"I guess a heart attack."

Jason Overly had always been an organized man and left a file—"in the event of my demise"—to be accessed only by Silvia Lewis. Before the trip down to St. Croix, she opened the document and verified his wishes. She also found his security codes and access protocols, which they would use to remove traces of Purple Frog from his computer systems.

Alan told the doctor, "He wanted to be cremated. Where can I have that done?"

"I know the best place. I'll call them and you should take the body there."

They did so, then made their way to Jason's home, Sugar Ridge.

Doris met them and cried openly. "Is Jason really gone?"

Alan sighed. "I'm afraid so."

In accordance with his wishes, Jason's ashes were scattered at sea in the same general area as he had disbursed his wife's remains. His daughters, their husbands, and his one grandchild traveled with Doris on a motor launch. About fifty friends from the island, from Avanch, and from other parts of the world joined a flotilla of small craft, which accompanied him on his final journey. The overseas attendees included Stavros Halkias, who had flown from Greece, and Henry Julong. Silvia and Alan motored out over the waves in a separate boat.

When they reached the area where they would conduct the ceremony and scatter Jason's ashes, a tropical rainstorm came out of nowhere and drenched the party for a few minutes. But the rain stopped, and after the brief ceremony, the flotilla started to return to shore. The sun emerged, and three rainbows arced into the sea behind them.

The following day, Silvia and Alan flew back to Virginia and met with Donna.

"We need to debrief on the attack here," Alan said, "but before we start that, I have bad news, Donna."

She looked at him, wondering what would come next.

"Our operative in Nasran who was supposed to meet Angkasa when she arrived by train," he said, "says that she was apprehended by the FSB and they carried her to a waiting helicopter."

"Dead?" Donna asked.

"No. The way they carried her indicated she was unconscious. Anyway, he found out that the chopper flew her to Moscow, and a contact there believes they took her to Lefortovo."

She groaned. "God help her."

"He reported that a few days later, the body of an Asian woman was removed from the prison and sent to a local mortuary. He gained access to it and texted us a picture. It was her."

Donna kept silent, remembering the Asia woman she had become fond of. Angkasa had been difficult to manage, but she was one of Donna's team members, and she felt responsible for her death.

"Did she suffer much?"

"The contact says she showed no physical signs of torture. The mortuary report indicated that some sort of poison was the cause of death. That's all we know."

They sat quietly for a minute, then Alan asked about the gang that had attacked them.

"While you were in St. Croix," she said, "we traced the leader's group back to a farm—really a training camp—in Indiana. Paul flew out and checked the site. The leader of the attackers was Tish Richey. Ex special forces, one of the few women who were in that service. She kept her records hidden, but we found them."

Donna did not need notes for the discussion.

"Paul retrieved her laptop and brought it back. Ching is having a field day with it. She had a detailed history of all their projects."

"They were obviously mercenaries," Alan said, "but do we know who they were working for?"

"Yes. Ching discovered that immediately. It was the FSB."

"It figures. They captured Angkasa and found our location from her. Our new president of the Russian Federation is at the bottom of this."

Silvia stared at the glass of water on her desk. Since the attack, she had ceased drinking coffee. "I think it's time we had an even newer president in Russia. I want Boris Menklov dead. Alan and Donna, put a plan together."

Boris Menklov looked around the presidential office that his predecessor, Dimitri Chekov, had occupied just a few weeks before. The furniture was heavy and dark, and the walls were painted a light brown. The drapes across the windows were also dark and old.

I need to change this room, he thought. *Something lighter, happier, perhaps more European and less Russian.*

A knock at his door brought him back from his thoughts.

"Enter." The door opened and Colonel Lomonosov strode into the room.

"Well?"

The FSB colonel looked down. "We have not heard from the American contractor."

"Explain."

"Their leader, a woman, communicated that they were in position and about to launch their attack on this Purple Frog organization."

"And?"

"That was a week ago. I have received no further communication."

The new president sighed. "Then it failed?"

"Very likely, sir."

"But we knew everything about them. The numbers, those who would be armed. You said the Richey group was skilled and had more than enough resources. How could they have failed?"

"Some of the information we uncovered from the prisoner was vague. Unfortunately, she also died more rapidly than we expected. But we found out a lot."

Menklov believed the man was evading his question.

"So what do we do now, Colonel? They are certainly not fools and will know that it was probably a Russian operation. They'll come for me next."

There was another knock on the door.

"Damn," the Russian president said, showing his anger. "Is it Kurskiy Train Station?"

Before the president could call out, the door opened and three soldiers with AK74Ms entered, followed by the head of the FSB.

Menklov snarled," What do you want, Director?"

"Mr. President, I have disturbing news about the death of President Chekov. I took the liberty of rerunning the autopsy. A more thorough autopsy."

Menklov glared at the man and felt a trickle of sweat slide down his back. "Why did you do that?"

The FSB director did not respond to Menklov's question. "The new autopsy indicates he was poisoned, sir."

The president hesitated, then said, "Rubbish. He had a food and drink taster. How could he have been poisoned?"

The director looked down at a notepad he held, but clearly knew the answer already. "The poison was in the vodka that he drank on the night of his death."

Menklov paused and the head of the FSB continued.

"The guard says you brought him a bottle on the night he died. As a gift."

Menklov flew into a rage. "Are you insane, Director? I am the president. You can't barge in here and accuse me of murdering Dimitri Chekov."

"But I have more, sir. We analyzed and found traces of the poison in the bottle."

The president was now openly sweating. "I drank from it as well. It did not kill me, nor even make me ill."

"We also have the security tapes. They show you consumed only a small quantity, as did his taster. The toxin used needs a lot more than that. And the victim must have an existing heart problem. President Chekov had that condition. You do not."

Menklov realized he had been caught and assumed he now had to find a way out. "Anyway, Director, who cares? I am president now. What do you want? I assume this is not an arrest but an extortion."

"Mr. President, it is an arrest."

Menklov laughed. "That is not going to happen. I relieve you of your command."

He turned to Colonel Lomonosov, who stood beside him.

"Place the director under arrest."

The colonel hesitated. His next move had a fifty-fifty chance of having him either promoted or jailed. Or even killed.

The FSB director said," Colonel, hand your pistol to the president."

"What?"

"Hand your pistol to the president."

The colonel did so and Menklov took it without understanding what was happening.

The director signaled to the lead soldier, who fired his rifle from the hip. A burst of four rounds left his weapon and killed the newly inaugurated Russian president instantly.

"He resisted arrest," the director said. "He had a gun. You had no choice, soldier. Well done."

Chapter Twenty-Nine

An hour later, the FSB director made an encrypted telephone call to a number that could have been anywhere in the world. Donna Strickland answered her phone.

The director was brief. "President Menklov resisted arrest, and, as you requested, is no longer with us."

"And the other matter?"

The head of the FSB spoke confidently. "I am in contact with the commandant of Penal Colony 2 in Pokrov. He is arranging for Anton Lanski's release and his secure carriage to Moscow. I'll assist him to the presidency. I hope you are happy with all this."

"I'll check his progress."

"And I'll check my account to verify you have paid me what we agreed. I trust you are not going to cheat me."

"I'll put the transfer through as soon as we end this call. Half now and half when Lanski takes power."

Donna hung up and called the voicemail of Purple Frog's head of finance.

"Hi, Sid. Send one million dollars to this account in the Cayman Islands." She rattled off a sort code and account number for the director's offshore holdings.

It was 5:00 a.m., and she had taken the call from her apartment living room. She padded back into the bedroom and looked at the man sleeping peacefully in her bed. He was a recent conquest, and she was happy with their relationship. He stirred, blinked, and said, "You're up early. What time is it?"

Although the call with the Russian had been audio only, Donna had felt that she had to dress for it, so she had pulled on a loose bathrobe. She now removed it and joined the naked man in her bed.

"It's only five o'clock," she said. "What should we do until it's time to get up?"

"I have a great idea."

Over the next month, Silvia and Alan held multiple calls with the new leaders and established a protocol that everyone was comfortable with. What the leaders did in their own countries was up to them, but signs of aggression beyond their territorial boundaries were not acceptable. The death of Boris Menklov did not go unnoticed, and with this clandestine organization's track record of eliminating their predecessors, the leaders harbored a fear of stepping over the line. They had realistic concerns about ending up dead.

Menklov's place had been taken by Anton Laski, the head of the opposition party in Russia, a man previously imprisoned by Chekov. On his release, he made pacts with the FSB director and the military. He scheduled open elections and was expected to become the newest president by a landslide.

The promises made by each country's president were slowly implemented and four months later, Alan and Silvia met to discuss progress.

Alan looked up from his laptop. "It's better than I dared hope. Iran and North Korea have ceased nuclear weapons development and allowed inspections by the International Atomic Energy Agency. So far, they seem to be living up to their pledges. Both countries are concentrating their efforts on addressing their local economies and making good advances."

"Russia?" Silvia asked.

"Laski is following through on Menkov's retreat from Ukraine, including Crimea. Half the troops are already out and the agreed ceasefire is holding."

"China?"

"The press just reported that they have officially recognized Taiwan as a sovereign country and have started the withdrawal of their forces in the South China Sea."

Silvia sat back and picked up a cup of coffee, having returned to her old habit. "Wow. It's working."

Alan looked up from his laptop again. "Yes, but it's tragic that we lost Jason, Angkasa, Neville, and Mary."

Silvia was about to say that four lives lost to enable what they had put in place was a small price to pay, but she paused to think. *No, it's not. When the press reports a hundred dead from an attack in Ukraine or Syria, or wherever, it's just a statistic. These four people were family. This was personal. This was a personal loss. This was different.*

Alan waited a brief moment, then said, "So, what does Purple Frog do next?"

"We monitor the situation and make modifications when necessary. It's going to be an ongoing fight. Every one of the four is going to keep looking for ways to thwart what we have done, so we'll be kept busy outwitting them. And in the short term, we need to finalize our plans for a new location."

Alan decided it was time to broach another subject. "There's something that I haven't told you."

"Yes?"

"In the early days of Operation Switch, I was very troubled about it and decided to share with Jess. I realized that I needed to tell her everything about Purple Frog, and I did. It was her support that helped me pull it off."

Silvia laughed. "Funny. After Jason's death, I did the same with Brian." She took a breath. "Let's have a quiet dinner, the four of us. We have a lot of issues we'll be facing over the next few years, and we'll need all the support from our partners that we can get."

Outside their offices, the sun was shining and the weather was warm. The race for election of the U.S. president was also heating up.

Chapter Thirty

It was mid-November. The leaves had fallen and the weather was gray and wet. But Fred Shidler was excited. He had an exclusive. It would be the first interview with the newly re-elected president of the United States, Bill Draper. Fred would question the president in a live broadcast for his *Government 2.0* program.

Conducting the program live meant that Shidler had no ability to edit the recording later, correcting any errors or gaffes on his part or on the part of the leader of the free world. He was conscious of the fact that if he made any serious mistakes, these would be obvious to a vast audience in real-time. His credibility would be shattered. If he pushed the president too far, he would be blacklisted. If he was too soft, his ratings would suffer as the other networks pilloried him. He knew the risks, but was confident in his ability to pull off the historic broadcast.

His crew had set up in the White House dining room, close to the Oval Office, and Fred was going over his notes. Unlike most of his interviews, the list of questions he would ask had been provided to the president and his staff in advance, and negotiations about what would be included and what would not had been carried out to keep the dialogue supportive of the administration, but still interesting to the viewers.

The president's chief of staff had insisted on a section of how the world had suddenly become so much more peaceful under Draper's watch, and this had been a major factor in the president's campaign success.

"Good evening, Mr. President," he began, "and may I congratulate you on your recent re-election."

Draper showed his expensive dental implants in his characteristic wide smile. "Thank you, Fred."

The interview proceeded well for the first fifteen minutes and Fred decided that now was the time to ask the $64,000 question. "So, Mr. President, over many decades, the United States has confronted challenges from a range of countries, but four of these have provided the highest levels of threat. Then, six months ago, the men leading each of America's major enemies died within a week or two. Two were the result of accidents, one was assassinated, and the fourth, Chekov, was initially thought to have suffered a heart attack, but it was later confirmed that he had been murdered by the man who attempted to take his role as president. This seems an amazing set of coincidences. Did the United States have anything to do with them?"

This was a prepared and agreed question, and the president had a prepared answer. "Certainly not. I've been asked about this dozens of times over the past six months, and my response has not changed. The United States and my administration have a clear policy. We do not involve ourselves in regime change. Presidents do not condone assassinations."

"The Russia situation seems straightforward, but did anyone claim responsibility for the Chinese president's assassination?"

Draper had memorized his answer for this question. "The man who is now running the country tells me that he believes it was a separatist group in Western China that orchestrated the killing."

"So, are the new leaders more attuned to working with the West?"

"Absolutely."

Shidler now moved to his next prepared question." You must be elated that over the past six months, each one of the four countries has lowered the heat dramatically. Talk of a third world war is behind us. How did you pull that off?"

"Well, let me tell you about a dream I had some months ago." He proceeded to tell the interviewer about the vivid dream in which his chief of staff briefed him on a global stand-down of America's enemies.

"And then a few months ago, the dream became a reality. Perhaps I have a gift. Perhaps God is supporting me. It certainly helped with my campaign."

You probably wouldn't have been elected if it hadn't been for this reversal, thought Shidler.

"But what role did the U.S. have in this? It's hard to believe it was all just coincidental. Four major leaders and their deputies die, new people take control, and their first act is to pull back potential and actual military operations."

The president was ready for this question. "It wasn't easy, but it comes from displaying strength. The deaths were coincidental, as we discussed, but the current players all know that America is strong, and they're afraid to mess with us. I've called each of them several times and we've had useful dialogues. They respect me and my administration, and more than that, they fear the U.S. military and our nuclear dominance."

"How will this change the world order and affect our military expenditure? If the threat has lessened, can we assume that the United States will cut back our spending?"

The president took a breath. This was not the wording of the question he had agreed to answer. "Perhaps you could rephrase that, Fred."

Shidler realized the president was avoiding a response and his expertise and insight kicked in. "Of course, sir." He paused for effect, then asked, "Will Congress vote to reduce our military budgets?"

"No. As a matter of fact, we shall be increasing them."

Fred was shocked. "Increase? How can you justify that?" This was not an agreed question.

Bill Draper was on a roll, though. "Good question. Our enemies have shown they are weak. They fear us, and we shall take advantage of that dynamic." As an afterthought, he added, "Each of the leaders is acting as though I have some magical power over him. Ha. Perhaps I do."

"How will the U.S. take advantage of this power?" Another query that was not in the agreed set. An aide signaled frantically to the president, cautioning him not to answer, but the commander of the armed forces ignored him.

"We'll show them the force of the United States of America. Within the next week, I will be ordering troop movements into each of the four axis countries to work with local officials to ensure their promises are kept. We will use this opportunity to increase our world dominance."

Shidler was aghast. "You're sending troops into these regions? Will they accept that?"

"My vice president and I have discussed this at length. We're in full agreement on the strategy. We have superior nuclear weaponry, and I have told our enemies that we are prepared to deploy it. We have been good guys for too long. Our adversaries think we are weak, and I'll show them that we're not. Oh, we'll also need more soldiers at home to quash any riots or protests. Some Americans may not agree with our policies."

It had never happened previously, but Fred Shidler was at a loss for words.

Draper filled the void. "The rain hasn't passed yet, and I see many days ahead before the sun comes out."

Silvia watched Shidler's interview with the U.S. president as it aired and shook her head. The president's rhetoric displayed what she had feared.

The program wrapped up, and five minutes later, the phone, used for calls with Tina Graham, rang.

"Hi, Tina," Silvia said.

"Hi, Leslie."

For years, Silvia had used the pseudonym, but now, she decided to share her real name with the CIA director.

"It's about time I told you my real name. It's Silvia."

"It's great to meet you, Silvia," Tina said with a laugh.

"So, what's going on in the CIA today?"

"Lots of things. Did you see the Shidler interview? It just finished."

"I saw it."

"And?"

Tina did not wait for Silvia to answer. "I was appalled that he went public with this. His election win was only confirmed a week ago, and since then, he has made himself clear. America will move into the global power vacuum and increase its world position."

Silvia had not shared with Tina the role Purple Frog had had in the regime change, but she was sure that Tina suspected they had played a major part in that.

"It's a pity that, when the world looks like it has solved a lot of its war-like issues, the U.S. decides to take advantage and raise the threat level again," Silvia continued.

"I agree. I was summoned to the Oval Office and instructed to put together plans to support a string of offensives. President Draper also talked about merging the CIA and FBI and adding a military contingent."

"And?"

"I resigned. In fact, I challenged the president, and he became angrier than I have ever seen him. He was on the point of firing me, but I got in first."

"So, you're unemployed?"

"I am."

"There's an independent spy agency I know that might have an opening."

She and Tina talked for a few more minutes, then ended the call.

Silvia poured her eighth cup of coffee for the day and made an internal call. Shortly afterward, Vivienne La Croix knocked and entered her office.

"Bonjour, Silvia," she said.

"Bonjour, Vivienne. Tell me what you have."

The French woman looked around her. "We are in your office, not the conference room. And Alan is not here. This is not usual. What's different?"

Silvia ignored her question. "I'll repeat, what do you have for me?"

"A lot. There's much I found about him, and I have put together a very detailed file."

Vivienne rattled off details of the target's educational background, his career history, his family, and his politics.

"That's fine, but can we achieve leverage on the man?"

"Absolutely. Ching hacked into his bank statements, tax returns, and emails. We uncovered significant gambling activity. He owes some bad people a lot of money. Judy traced a couple of offshore accounts with transfers from Colombia, so it's likely that cartel funds are involved. Probably funds to help pay his debts. If this information is released, he'll go down for corruption and worse."

"Good. So, we have him. We have proof."

"Absolutely."

Vivienne La Croix, being French, had struggled with some of the idiosyncrasies of American culture and politics. She crossed her legs and sat back in her chair. "I'm surprised that you wanted a profile on this man. All the others we've developed have been foreign citizens, usually in enemy countries. This is the first U.S. citizen you've asked me to research."

"You're right."

"Interesting. This man is a senior member of the federal government. He is the speaker of the House of Representatives." She adjusted her eyeglasses. "It's really an odd thing. When I researched the position of the speaker, I noticed that he is second in line to become American president after the vice president. But only if they die…"

"Exactly." The Galactic Empress nodded with a grim smile. Then she reached over to her intercom and spoke into it. "Alan, please join me."

As she waited for her head of operations, Silvia looked out of the window of her office. It was late fall, and cold for the time of year. But the sun was emerging from the dark clouds surrounding the building.

The End of the Purple Frog Series

About the Author:

Harry Bunn has traveled to over fifty countries worldwide, and has resided in Sydney, Australia; London, England; and Princeton, NJ. He founded an international marketing consulting firm focused on the technology sector, managed it for thirty years, and is now retired in St. Croix in the U.S. Virgin Islands, where he lives with his wife, Jackie. They have two sons, James and Nicholas. Harry has taken up writing since his retirement, with a variety of themes, but his focus has been on a series of thrillers—Purple Frog.

Contact him at harrybunnauthor@gmail.com, or check out his website for video trailers for each book and access to Amazon listing sites for each.

https://lifemadesimple.store

Other Purple Frog Books

Purple Frog (Book 1)

Jason Overly, a technology billionaire, funds a daring rogue operation devoted to world peace. This international team employs unorthodox methods, including hacking, blackmail, extortion, and occasionally, murder. The group has been given the name Purple Frog after a little-known frog that spends most of its time underground, out of sight, emerging only for two weeks each year. Keeping below the radar is key to Purple Frog's success, but a plot to assassinate the new president of the European Union calls for more direct action and the risk of discovery.

MetalWorks (Book 2)

Frederik Verwoerd is successful and rich, but wants more. His desire is to become a major player on the world stage, and he decides that his South African armament company, MetalWorks, will develop a new weapon of mass destruction, which he will sell to the highest bidder. The weapon is neither nuclear, chemical, nor biological, but can destroy an army of five thousand tanks in the field, or even a major city. To demonstrate its power, he targets a well-protected symbol of the United States and will telecast its destruction live.

It falls to Purple Frog, a private and clandestine organization, to stop him, but to do so, Purple Frog must reveal its existence to the CIA. However, it is already facing a threat from the Russian president, who wants to locate and punish the organization.

Brotherhood of the Skull (Book 3)

Outside Washington, DC, one million armed white supremacists have assembled to march on the capital and seize power. They are led by Gideon Page, a charismatic but ruthless white supremacist, and Jonathan Greer, a televangelist. They have a symbol for their insurrection: an ancient skull previously owned by Adolf Hitler. A rogue U.S. senator, Jeffrey Kendall, has teamed up with them and expects to become the new president of the United States after the Brotherhood of the Skull overthrows the present elected government.

Law enforcement is hamstrung by legalities and political correctness, but the clandestine Purple Frog organization has no such limitations and moves to thwart this attack on American democracy.

Citadel of Yakutsk (Book 4)

"The Citadel is the real threat." The dying words of the CIA Chief of Station in Moscow are cryptic, but no one knows what his message means. Yakutsk is a remote city in Siberia. It boasts the coldest weather of any city on the planet, and is home to a clandestine facility in subterranean caves deep beneath the conurbation. This secret metropolis is the headquarters of Alexi Rackov, a Russian general who has developed a plan to expand Russian territory by invading eight countries and bringing eighty-eight million European citizens under Russian hegemony. While there are rumors about such a site, these only identify its name: the Citadel. Its location and mission are known only to Rackov and Dobry Petrovski, the Russian president.

In the United States, Purple Frog is a secret organization established by Jason Overly, a tech billionaire, with the mission to foster world peace. Though Purple Frog parallels the CIA and MI6, it operates outside the rules and political correctness of these intelligence organizations. It will face its greatest challenge as its small team strives to prevent the annexation of these Eastern European countries.

Flag Eight (Book 5)

A new president in Venezuela, Mateo Videgain, is facing a multitude of problems, including a collapsed economy. He regards the United States as a major reason for this and his main enemy, deciding on a bold plan to consolidate his place in history.

Just 520 miles to the north is the U.S. territory of St. Croix, and Videgain decides to invade and occupy the island.

All hell breaks loose as, with help from Russia, his helicopters, warships, and troops attack. When the locals fight back against his vastly superior forces, the battle is short and the Venezuelans take control.

Few countries have been ruled by seven different nations, but over the five hundred and twenty-eight years since St. Croix's discovery by Christopher Columbus, it has been a territory of Spain, France, the Netherlands, England, the Knights of Malta, Denmark, and most recently, the U.S. In total, seven flags have flown over the island. The Venezuelan president raises his flag over the territory—*flag eight*.

He has not, however, factored in that Jason Overly, who has a home on the island, is also the head of a clandestine intelligence operation called Purple Frog, which will do whatever is necessary to stop the plans of the Venezuelan president.

To Venice with Love (Book 6)

Alan Harlan and his new wife, Jess, embark on their honeymoon to a Greek island, but they encounter an old enemy and a Saudi prince, who have deployed a bioweapon on an ecologically advanced super yacht. Alan and Jess find themselves on the vessel's maiden voyage from Athens to Venice, discover the plot, and need to identify which of the passengers or crew will be responsible for triggering the device on their arrival in Venice.

Alan is head of operations for Purple Frog, a clandestine organization mirroring the CIA and MI6, but with fewer constraints. He brings many of Purple Frog's resources into play as they battle the forces striving to destroy this romantic Italian city's population, together with one million visiting tourists.

Delete Code (Book 7)

Mike Young, a computer hacker, develops a set of malware that can delete every file and piece of software from any computer that he targets. Initially, he sees this as an approach to extort money, but others see it as a powerful weapon of destruction. After successful demonstrations of the code's power, a major enemy of the United States develops a plan to use it to further its goal of world domination. The cybersecurity forces in government and the corporate world find themselves unable to counter the threat, so it falls to the hackers and field operations staff of Purple Frog to isolate and remove the danger.

Brisa's Grief (Book 8)

The head of a drug cartel, a billionaire, a spy's wife, and a killer experience grief and resolve it in different ways.

A DEA team raids the headquarters of a South American drug cartel, but things don't go as planned, and the daughter of the cartel chief seeks revenge on the United States. She develops a new narcotic, which she plans to release, killing several million Americans.

With political tensions running high, the U.S. governmental agencies are unable to act, and the task of preventing the disaster falls to Purple Frog, a clandestine organization devoted to world peace, but without the constraints of conventional intelligence organizations.

Assault and Battery (Book 9)

November Swan is the third richest person in the world, but his portfolio of companies is turning sour. To tackle this threat, he decides to go "all in," acquiring a startup company that is developing next-generation, solid-state batteries for electric vehicles.

His plan requires access to rare earth components, which are needed for large-scale manufacturing. These are located only in China.

Having always skirted the law and regulations, Swan pushes into more criminal acts to achieve his objectives, including a deal with China that puts the U.S. economy and its security in peril.

The Purple Frog team is tasked with stopping him.

Made in the USA
Columbia, SC
08 August 2023